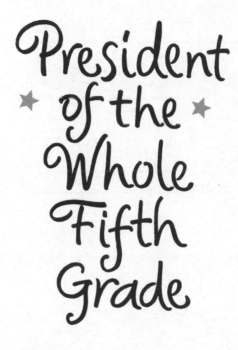

President
of the
Whole
Fifth
Grade

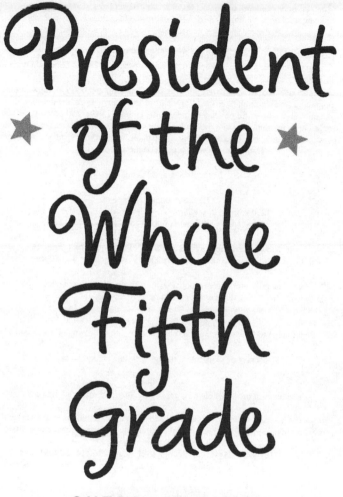

President of the Whole Fifth Grade

SHERRI WINSTON

LITTLE, BROWN AND COMPANY
New York   Boston

Copyright © 2010 by Sherri Winston
Excerpt from *President of the Whole Sixth Grade* copyright © 2015 by Sherri Winston

Little, Brown and Company

Hachette Book Group
1290 Avenue of the Americas, New York, NY 10104
Visit us at lb-kids.com

Little, Brown and Company is a division of Hachette Book Group, Inc.
The Little, Brown name and logo are trademarks of Hachette Book Group, Inc.

The publisher is not responsible for websites (or their content) that are not owned by the publisher.

First Paperback Edition: October 2012
First published in hardcover in October 2010 by Little, Brown and Company

Library of Congress Cataloging-in-Publication Data
Winston, Sherri.
President of the whole fifth grade / by Sherri Winston. — 1st ed.
p. cm.
Summary: To gain leadership skills needed to run a cupcake-baking empire when she grows up, Brianna runs for president of the fifth grade—expecting little competition—until a new girl enters the race.
ISBN 978-0-316-11432-5 (hc) / ISBN 978-0-316-11433-2 (pb)
[1. Elections—Fiction. 2. Leadership—Fiction. 3. Baking—Fiction. 4. Schools—Fiction.] I. Title.
PZ7.W7536Pr 2010
[Fic]—dc22
2010006366

20 19 18 17

RRD-C

Printed in the United States of America

To Lauren, Kenya, Daelyn, Stevie,
Evan, Javonne, and Vincent—the
beautiful people who keep my
heart young. I love you!

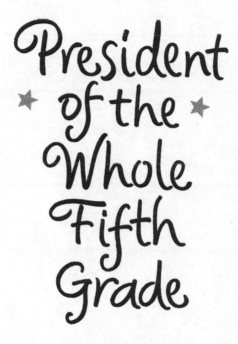

1

Declaration of Independence!

My name is Brianna Justice, and I want to be president of the whole fifth grade!

That is my "declaration."

As in, "I do declare that *I will be president* of the whole entire fifth grade at Orchard Park Elementary."

My aunt Tina says that if we want good things to happen we have to make them happen. Take action! State your plan out loud. **DECLARE!**

And I want good things to happen. I have BIG plans. I'm going to be a millionaire with my own cooking show on TV. Cupcakes are my specialty.

Aunt Tina also says that along with declaring your goal, you have to have a plan. Think about what you want, decide how you plan to get it, then write it down and keep notes along the way. That's how you make a plan. All really important, successful people do, she says. (Grandpa says if Aunt Tina had a husband instead of "just a career" maybe she wouldn't have time for so many plans. *Hmph!*) Anyway, ever since a certain hometown celebrity spoke to our class last January, I've known what I need to do. Here's my plan:

I live in Orchard Park, Michigan. We're not far from Detroit, Michigan. But Orchard Park is a suburb. That means unless you live here, you probably never heard of it. At least, not until my hero, Miss Delicious, became world-famous as a chef, author, TV-show host, and GAZILLIONAIRE. Miss Delicious grew up right here in Orchard Park.

And she even went to the same elementary school as me!

When she spoke to our fourth-grade class, she told us that she didn't think any of her success would have been possible had it not been for the skills she learned at our school.

But this is the most important thing she said:

"I honestly believe that if I hadn't been voted president of my fifth-grade class, if I hadn't learned how to manage my responsibilities back then and be a true leader, I don't know if any of this would have been possible."

So the best way for me to follow in her footsteps would be to become president of my fifth-grade class, too.

Ever since that day, every morning when I arrive at school, I pass through the front hallway where all the plaques hang or sit on shelves showing the names of all the fifth graders who have been president. And I say a tiny little prayer and run my fingers over Miss Delicious's name for good luck.

That same day I told my friends, basically our whole class, that I was going to be just like Miss Delicious. I was going to be a millionaire cupcake baker and sell tons of books and be wildly famous on television.

And the first step would be to become president of the fifth grade.

So you see, it is so totally obvious: I have to win the election.

All summer I planned. I've written speeches. I've

researched school-approved places for our class trip and other interests vital to our fifth-grade class.

Little did I know how much would change once school started up after summer break. My plan seemed to be going so well, *until*...

2

"The Redcoats Are Coming..."

...Until!

A tiny word, but it can be an ugly thing.

Like the way parents use it:

"No chocolate cake *until* you finish your broccoli."
Or... "No allowance *until* all your chores are finished!"
Or "You did what? Just wait *until* I tell your father, missy!"

See what I mean? *Until.* It's not hard to spell, but when it crashes into a kid's life, it can really wreck her day.

What had happened was: I was all set to take my rightful place in history as fifth-grade president at Orchard Park Elementary. Mrs. Nutmeg had asked the class to nominate the student or students worthy of being president. My friends nominated me and almost the whole class seconded it. Except the disgusting Back Row Boys. We had all known that Todd Hampton's fellow toadies would nominate him. *Hmph!* Like he could really win. He was still acting funky because while I was planning and plotting and waiting for my chance at the school elections, I took an afternoon off this summer to kick his butt in basketball. That's right. My all-girl team beat his all-boy team. It felt so good, I made up my own song:

Ah, ha, okay! The girls are better any day!

Yeah, I love that song. Todd, not so much.

So of course he was going to run against me, and of course he had no shot because, let's face it, everybody, Everybody, EVERYBODY knows I'm much better prepared than Todd and would make a much better president.

Except there was a new twist—the election wasn't just for each fifth-grade class to have its own president. Nuh-uh. This year, for the first time in Orchard Park Elementary history, there would be only ONE fifth-grade president.

President of the WHOLE fifth grade.

But the twists didn't stop there! Now, this year, not

only would the winner of the election be president of the whole fifth grade, he or she would be president of the whole school. If that wasn't enough to throw me for a loop, Dr. Beelie had won some kind of grant, which is a fancy teacher way of saying money—cash, moola, cheddar, ching-ching. So the new school president and president of the whole fifth grade would also have a HUGE responsibility: deciding how to use the $5,000 budget. Five thousand smackeroonies! The idea of being in charge of that kind of money made me light-headed with happiness.

My heart leapt at the news. Back when Miss Delicious spoke at our school, I thought I could be president of just my class, same as it had always been. But now that had changed. Was I ready for that big of a challenge? That kind of responsibility?

I couldn't help thinking about other challenges, other goals I'd had. Like the time I decided I needed to be the best free-throw shooter on our team. I'd written down my notes on how to stand, how to breathe, stuff coach had talked to me about, and stuff Dad helped me find online. That had been an important goal for me. And I did it!

So was I ready to be school president and president of the whole fifth grade?

YES! Yes, I was.

So bring it on. It would be even better than I had imagined. And I could just see me making my acceptance speech, that is, *until*...

Mrs. Gayle entered our classroom with a girl whose long, crinkly hair almost covered her face and said the words that will haunt me forever and ever. Mrs. Gayle said:

"Everyone, we have a new student. Please say hello to Jasmine Moon..."

ELECTION NOTEBOOK

(Mrs. Nutmeg says all of her students need to keep some kind of journal about the school elections, especially the candidates!)

Election Rules

- ⊗ Each of the five fifth-grade classes will have to pick two students. If more than two students get picked in one classroom, they have to have a mini-election called a "primary" to choose which two will run.

- ⊗ When each class has its two picks or candidates for president, those students compete against each other and all the other candidates. Whoever gets the most votes from kids from first grade to fifth grade wins!

- ⊗ The winner gets to go to Washington, D.C., to tour the *White House*, Principal Beelie told us.

- ⊗ What could be a better way to learn leadership skills and launch a mega-million-dollar empire than to be president of all the grades and all the kids at your school and go to the real White House?

3
War!

So, with only six weeks until the election a new girl just appears in fifth grade. It was like the time I fell off the jungle gym and landed flat on my back. It totally knocked the wind out of me! Because the new girl didn't just show up in our class. When she heard about the elections for president, she *nominated herself!*

F-O-O-L-I-S-H-N-E-S-S!

Later that same afternoon, on the playground, it went down just like this:

We were at the corner court. No boys or geeks allowed. Toady Todd Hampton had kicked his basketball into our court. Did I forget to mention, we don't allow amphibians, either? We just kicked it back to him and ignored him as he made faces and hopped around like a true toad.

I was having one of those moments when everything feels so bright, so amazing, it's like you're outside your own body looking at the world. I saw myself, short, with curly brown hair that reached my shoulders; Lauren, tall, with her long blond hair; Sara, with her slightly slanted eyes and pale beige skin that came from having a Korean mother and black father; and Rebecca, who everyone called Becks for short, who was a little bit soft, a little bit round, but one of the sweetest people ever.

My friends. We all had so many plans for our futures. We needed each other. We were like the ingredients to an awesome cake recipe—and I was the egg. Hey, if you're baking, you need the egg. The egg is what holds all that flour, sugar, salt, and butter together.

"Earth to Bree," Sara said, tossing her long and straight dark hair. "Are you plotting world domination again?" She wrinkled her nose when she said "world domination." Sara was the big nonfighter in the group. To her, world domination probably seemed crazy and wrong. (But not to me!)

We all laughed.

Okay, I'll admit it. At times I liked thinking about having fame and fortune. Throwing my head back like a mad scientist, I said in my best hungry-for-power voice, "One day I will rule the world... *waa-haa-ha!*" (The wild laugh at the end is key!!!)

We all laughed again. We were still laughing when Lauren said, "Look who thinks she can just sashay over here uninvited."

Jasmine Moon.

I gave Lauren a jab in the ribs. Maybe we were being a little hasty.

The new girl was tall with long hair. But, as Todd liked to point out, just about everyone was taller than me.

She stopped right in front of me. She tossed her extra-crinkly hair. She stuck out her hip and put one hand on it. Then she blazed me with her extra-white smile. Hoping I'd brushed and flossed extra well that morning, I tried to match her with my own.

"So you're Brianna." She said it like she was singing.

I reached out to shake her hand. Yeah, I know, hand-shaking is sort of weird among kids, but my b-ball coach from the summer acted like hand-shaking was maybe one of the most important things in life. And I have to admit, you can figure out a lot about people by how they shake your hand.

So, with my hand hanging out there, I said, "Hey, so you're Jasmine Moon."

Um, just so you know, she didn't shake my hand right away. Now that tells you something right there.

"I've heard so much about you. I really hope we get to be great friends!"

Yep, that's what she said, but my hand, oh, yeah, still hanging.

"Well, Orchard Park is a really cool school. I think you'll like it a lot." She finally took my hand. Her fingers were cold and her handshake was real limp.

I saw Becks exhale. She'd probably been holding her breath. She did that when she got nervous. Lauren, however, was in her warrior pose — feet firmly planted shoulder distance apart, shoulders back, chest out. Remember when I said Sara didn't much like fighting? Well, Lauren was a karate expert!

I almost laughed. Lauren looked like she'd karate-chop Jasmine Moon's guts out if the girl tried to shake her hand with those cold, limp fingers. Becks's eyes grew large and round, and Sara's eyes seemed to bounce from Lauren to Jasmine Moon.

"Um, you know, Brianna, I hope your feelings didn't get hurt in class today. The whole election thing. No offense. I've just always wanted to be class president, but I'm sure I don't stand a chance against you."

"You've got that right," said Lauren.

Oh, snap, crackle, and pop!

Sara and Becks covered their mouths with their hands. Their eyes were all big and round as if they couldn't imagine Lauren had really said such a thing.

And for just a second, the golden rays of sunshine oozing out of Jasmine Moon's toothy grin turned icy cold. She turned toward Lauren as if she was ready to get something started.

So I said, "What Lauren meant was it might be tough, you know, running for president of the whole fifth grade, since you don't really know anybody here. But good luck anyway."

See, those leadership skills were kicking in already, and I hadn't even won yet—not technically.

She turned back to me and fixed her face. Now the smile was as bright and glowy as ever.

"Well, like I was saying, no offense. May the best girl...um, I mean candidate, win." Then she swung around, tossed her long, crinkly hair over her shoulder, and strolled away.

But not before giving me... *a look*.

"Did you see that?" I asked. Sara, Lauren, and Becks shook their heads.

Becks said, "See what?"

"That... *look*. She gave me a weird look."

Sara let out a long sigh like maybe she'd been holding her breath, too. "Well, she's got guts, I'll say that. Maybe...I don't know. Maybe she'll be okay. I mean, I don't want her for president, but maybe we'll get to like her."

See, that's why I like Sara, bless her heart. She always wants everyone to be friends and for everything to be sweet as pie. Of course, as a dedicated leader, I wanted the same thing.

But I couldn't help thinking about how Lauren had reacted. Lauren acted like Jasmine Moon was meant to be her boxing partner. Had Lauren sensed something? Was it the same thing I'd just seen in Jasmine Moon? That look she'd given me, like she thought I wouldn't be ANY competition—AT ALL!!!

With Jasmine Moon running for president, suddenly I wasn't so sure...about anything!

ELECTION NOTEBOOK

The Revolutionary War

We're supposed to write a few paragraphs about what it would have been like to be a leader during the American Revolution. (Mrs. Nutmeg says if it's not in our own words that "there'll be consequences." Trust me, I don't want to find out what they are.)

So here goes:

Americans wanted change. That's why they left Britain. You know, that place where they speak English, too, but theirs sounds really funny.

Anyway, people left because they wanted freedom. They wanted change. And I guess they wanted tea, too, because they came to Boston and had a big ol' tea party.

Well, I like freedom, democracy, and iced tea!

So, in conclusion, if I would have been in charge back then, I'd have thrown a big tea party, too. And I'd have told the British people to take a hike. You're not the boss of us Americans anymore!!!

4
Victoria Woodhull for U.S. President!

Tuesday, the next day, I awoke before my alarm went off. My room was on the second floor overlooking the backyard. A big oak tree with fat green leaves reached toward my window as though it were yawning. I stretched my limbs like the tree. Today was going to be great. Awesome, even!

After I brushed my teeth and washed my face, I sat on my bed and held Pig Pig in my lap. Pig Pig was the huge, pink ceramic piggy bank Grandpa gave me for Christmas when I was five. Sure, I had money in the bank—the bank where Sara's mom worked. But I kept money in Pig Pig, too. Lots of quarters and dimes and pennies. I liked to hear my change rattle in Pig Pig's big ol' pink belly.

And every morning, I gave Pig Pig a little shake. You know, for good luck.

Something told me I was going to need a double shake today.

And I was right!

At lunchtime in the cafeteria, our lunch choices were between barfilicious meatloaf or totally repugnant mac 'n' cheese. Our fourth-grade teacher was a beast about vocabulary words. I loved learning words like *repugnant*. It sounds like what it means: truly disgusting.

I saw a kid from another fifth-grade class fake sticking his finger down his throat and pretending to gag. Another girl from my art class whispered, "My father works for the health department. I wish he could come here and shut this place down! We deserve better choices!"

I'd seen enough. Grabbing an apple and a carton of milk, I rushed toward our usual table.

Then three kids blocked my path. It was Annie Darling, the school's most well-known journalist, and her cameraman, a nerdy boy who didn't talk. Following them was a semi-creepy girl I'd known since kindergarten named Tabitha Handy.

Annie Darling said, "The whole school is talking

about it. Care to comment?" She held her notebook at the ready.

I pretended not to know what she meant.

"You know, the new girl. Jasmine Moon? She really wants in on the election; and even though she's only been here a day, she's already getting lots of attention."

Then Tabitha Handy, who'd been basically trying to be just like me since kindergarten, freaked me out when she said:

"I'm going to work on Jasmine Moon's campaign."

Huh? She said it as if working on Jasmine Moon's campaign was like the coolest thing ever. Good grief! In kindergarten, Tabitha sat right next to me. If I sipped from my milk carton, so did she. If I drew with a red crayon, so did she. First grade was no different. By second grade she was going around telling people her name was really Brianna Justice, too.

I mean, come on, people. Now, after years of trying to be just like me, even Tabitha Handy was in a total daze over the New Girl???

Foolishness. I pushed past Tabitha, Annie Darling, and Nerdy Boy.

I tried not to shudder as I slid into my seat at the

lunchroom table. A true leader doesn't let her fear show, right? And the truth was, the whole competition for president thing was making my insides shake.

Becks slid into the seat next to mine. Lauren and Sara sat across from us. Lauren was stretching her arms with her fingers locked together. She looked as if she were getting ready for a karate match. Becks took two long blasts from her asthma inhaler. Her round cheeks were pinkish and she looked excited.

She said, "Hey you guys, guess what?" And just like Becks, before any of us could say a word, she kept on talking. "I saw Jeremy Ross earlier. He said his father works for a publishing company and he'd heard about my summer trip to Brazil—Jeremy, I mean, not his dad. Anyway, Jeremy said that his dad's company pays good money for well-written stories by kids, so I should write about my trip. But he said to write like it's fiction. As if it happened to someone else, like him. Jeremy, not his dad. Jeremy says if I write it, he'll make sure his dad reads it."

She let out a big exhale and sat back, her face shiny with excitement.

Poor Becks.

"You're kidding, right?" Lauren said and rolled her eyes.

Sara just shook her head.

"What?" said Becks.

I draped my arm across her shoulder. "Becks, Jeremy's dad doesn't work for any publisher person. He's a fireman. Remember in third grade when he came in on career day?"

"Then why . . ."

Lauren cut her off before Becks could finish her question. "Because Jeremy is in Mrs. Bigelow's class and that's the assignment she made when school first started."

"Jeremy probably blew it off and now he's desperate. He just wants you to do his homework," I said.

"You really think so?" she asked.

I nodded.

See, Becks was like that. She was the nicest, sweetest person in the world. But sometimes . . . well, I'd hate to think what might happen to her if she didn't have us watching her back.

Sara said, "Okay, now that that's settled, we really need to talk about this whole Jasmine Moon thing."

"She seemed nice on the playground," said Becks.

"Rebecca! Don't be a doof! She's totally trying to steal the election from Brianna," Lauren said.

Sara squinted and rubbed her forehead for a second, then said, "I'm worried. You should have been the easy favorite to be president of Mrs. Nutmeg's class. But now that it's between all the fifth grades and we have that new girl, and the word is that her dad is some kind of coach or something for the Pistons, well..."

None of us wanted to say anything after that.

Sara was right. Having a dad on the coaching staff for the Detroit Pistons was like being royalty. Girls would look up to her and guys would be in awe.

After a few seconds, Sara smiled.

"What?" I asked.

Sara raised her milk carton and said, "What are we worried about? We're the girls of the Woodhull Society!" Sara was right. We all smiled.

Sara's mom worked for a bank and helped us keep up with our own bank accounts so we could save our money. When we first started, she told us we needed a name for our group. For a while we didn't know what to call ourselves, then Mom and Aunt Tina took us to the museum and we saw an exhibit about great women. Well, one woman we learned about was Victoria Woodhull. She was once called "the queen of finance." And she was the first woman to run for president. Mom told us she would be the perfect role model for our money-saving club.

With our milk and juice cartons held high in the cafeteria, we cheered, "To the girls of the Woodhull Society!"

I got chills. Of course, I was a Woodhull girl. It was like an omen. Victoria Woodhull was the first woman to run for president of the United States. And she was smart about making and saving money. I wasn't the first girl to run for president at our school, but I could wind up being the first girl—the first kid ever—to be president of the whole school and not just one class.

And rich, too. Don't forget rich!

Lauren nodded and looked at me. "It will be just like we planned. First, you will become president of the whole fifth grade. We didn't spend all summer listening to you talk about the election and all that for nothing. You will be president. Then you will get your own **cupcake cooking show** and be a millionaire."

Hey, I liked the way that sounded!

I said to Lauren, "And one day you are going to be a famous Hollywood stuntwoman and then have your own TV show!"

Rebecca raised her milk carton to Sara. "You're going to be an Olympic horse rider and a millionaire business-woman."

We turned to Becks. "And if we can keep you away from scammers like Jeremy Ross, you'll be a totally famous author!"

"And...," we all said together, "be a millionaire!"

We laughed and said "cheers," bumping our milk cartons together.

Rebecca's round cheeks turned a brighter shade of pink after she took another pull on her inhaler. She was waving her hand, like she wanted to be called on in class or something.

"For goodness sake, Becks, stop raising your hand!" Lauren said with a laugh.

"Okay, okay. Can I just give Brianna one piece of advice?"

You know she didn't wait for anybody to answer her, right?

"Brianna, okay, you know we love you. But please

can you promise that you won't get too, too, *tooooooo* carried away with the election?"

Sara was nodding her head, her upturned brown eyes sparkling.

"She is right, you know? You do get..."

"Caught up!" Lauren finished the statement.

I batted my eyes dramatically. "Who me? *Moi?* I? Carried away?"

"CARRIED AWAY! Crazy for WORLD DOMINATION!!!" they all said at once. Then followed it up with a hearty, *"Waa-haaa-ha-ha!"*

We all burst out laughing. Okay, so sometimes I did get so excited about stuff that...well, I couldn't think about anything else. But who could blame me if that happened this time? We're talking about being president of the fifth grade, people.

We were still laughing and playing around when a shadowy movement caught my attention. The next thing I knew I was yelling:

"Whoa! There's a horse in my soup!"

5

Beware the Dark Horse!

The silhouette of a man on a horse appeared inside the cafeteria's double doors, right next to us.

Then, even though the man on the horse kept saying, "Whoa! Whoa! Whoa!" the horse kept whinnying and twisting around, and before I knew it...

Well, the horse trotted sideways, snorted, and *dunked his snout in my soup*.

I jumped backward and almost landed on the floor. Big Wally, a burly bully who used to take Becks's lunch money in third grade before Lauren used her karate training to kick his legs out from under him and pin him to the ground, looked like he'd seen not just a horse, but a ghost horse. The horse clattered over the tile floor. His tail swished. He looked nervous.

The cafeteria was what grown-ups call a solarium, but it sometimes felt more like an aquarium. It had a really high ceiling that went up like two, maybe three stories. And the roof part was made of glass so when it was sunny out, like today, the whole room was bright.

But it also made noise sound really loud. As if the glass top sealed all the yelling and squealing and goofing around tight inside, like closing a lid on a jar. When it got loud in here, it was really loud!

I realized it was Principal Beelie on the horse's back, dressed like George Washington. His big, round belly **jiggled** every time the horse reared up. I never pictured George Washington with a big, round belly.

And I never pictured him scared or sweaty either.

Principal Beelie was both.

The horse trotted forward, table and chair legs scraping the floor as kids slid over to make a path. I felt like I was right in the middle of some sort of reality show on TV. Beelie was sweating because I bet that George Washington wig made his head hot. Assistant Principal Smith popped out of nowhere making "nice doggy" sounds to the horse.

Sara made a disgusted sound. I looked at her and shrugged.

Rebecca said, "You aren't going to eat the rest of that soup, are you? It's full of horse germs!"

My mind flashed back to one of the "little-known facts" Mrs. Nutmeg had written on the blackboard: George Washington used to have people brush his horses' teeth. EVERY MORNING! I looked at Big Wally. I'd known that boy since forever and I knew for a fact he didn't brush his teeth every morning.

Snrt!

I guess that was horse for "get me back to the farm!" The animal trotted backward a few feet and snorted again.

Sara and I exchanged glances. Sara loved horses. She had horses. Sometimes when we hung out at her house, we'd ride them together. Sara hated to see animals in distress, and Dr. Beelie's horse was in distress big-time.

Sara leaned over and said, "This is terrible. That poor animal is frightened and Dr. Big Belly is too busy being president of the principals with his costume to care."

Sara could be pretty feisty when she got angry.

Assistant Principal Smith said, "Dr. Beelie wants all you boys and girls to give the fifth graders your utmost respect and attention as they plunge into their roles as junior decision makers. We..."

Right then the horse reared up and made a loud *WHEE-HEE-HEE-HEE!* And Dr. Beelie let out a loud "Yeow!"

And then out of nowhere... *SHE* appeared.

Jasmine Moon.

She just popped up and all of a sudden she was next to Dr. Beelie and the unhappy horse. Sara sprang to her feet. But before Sara could take a single step, Jasmine Moon placed her hand on the side of the horse's snout and gently rubbed. Then she stood on a chair and leaned forward. The horse actually lowered its head as if waiting for a secret.

Sara looked at me.

I looked at Sara.

Well, the next thing you know, the horse was all nice and Jasmine was all smiley like some kind of horse whisperer.

Foolishness, that's what it was!

Dr. Beelie almost fell off the saddle, then he said a bunch of stuff about how important the elections were to America and a bunch of other blah-blah-blah-ness... Then he said the *worst thing ever!*

Dr. Beelie looked at Jasmine and said:

"Young lady, I don't know what you just whispered to Mr. Lucky, but if you're as good with the students as you are with animals you could definitely wind up the president of the fifth grade!"

I felt like I had just gotten kicked by Mr. Lucky.

And if that wasn't bad enough, I was so flustered, I scooped up a spoonful of my soup and slurped it down.

"No!" cried all my friends.

Oh no!

Not only was it possible I might lose the most important election ever and wind up without important leadership skills and then of course be unable to run a big cupcake empire or get my own TV show, which would mean no millions. Now I might be dead any minute because I'd just slurped down a big spoonful of chicken noodles and horse slobber.

That night, after I'd brushed my teeth and gargled an

extra-long time to try and kill any stray horse cooties, I plopped onto the bed and fell back against my pillow.

All I ever wanted was to be a millionaire cupcake maker. And Miss Delicious had told me exactly how to do it when she spoke to our class last January.

"So why is it getting so hard, Pig Pig?"

Pig Pig's belly rumbled with shifting quarters and dimes and nickels and pennies, but his painted eyes did not blink. And his painted mouth did not speak.

This whole woman of big business thing might be harder than I thought. If I lose the election, could that really change my entire life plan? My future?

I fell asleep clutching Pig Pig to my chest and hoping for an answer that did not come in the night.

6

~~Vote for Brianna!~~
~~Sweet Justice~~
~~Pick Me~~
(HELP! We need a slogan!)

Elections were less than six weeks away.

November third.

The first Tuesday in November.

I was hanging upside down from a branch in my back-yard letting the blood pump into my brain. Around me, green leaves flapped like new dollar bills. I was thinking about Jasmine Moon when I heard loud snoring from the porch.

Grandpa!

As usual, he'd fallen asleep while he was supposed to be "supervising" us. I flipped down from the tree and went over to give him a shake.

"WHAT?" he shouted, sat up, and looked around like he was in combat and the enemy was shooting.

"Grandpa, you're...you know...snoring."

He frowned, shook his head, and grumbled, "You kids keep down your racket. Brianna, get in there and make sure them cupcakes don't burn!"

Oh, well, I needed to check my cupcakes anyway. Sara, Becks, and Lauren followed me into the kitchen. "It smells sooo good!" Lauren said.

"I bet this is how it smells at Miss Delicious's house all the time," Sara said.

I opened the oven carefully. I set the cupcake pan on the stovetop and then gently removed each cupcake and set them on the cooling rack.

I ☆ I ☆ I ☆ I

"No offense, but we're supposed to be working on your campaign strategy," Sara said.

"I am," I said as I scraped the sides of the mixing bowl. "I've been working on a new recipe for homemade chocolate frosting."

Sara rolled her eyes. She said, "A campaign strategy is

what people use to help them become president. Bree, your strategy would be the perfect way to show kids you are going to be a smart, funny, fair president who cares."

Lauren snorted and then tasted the frosting. "I think Bree's strategy should be to crush the competition. Coach always says 'go hard or go home'!"

"What does that even mean?" said Sara.

I couldn't help laughing. This was typical of those two. Lauren shot back, "It means forget all that fuzzy-wuzzy nicey-nice. The campaign should let everybody know that Brianna isn't playing around. And that she's willing to pound anyone who gets in her way."

"You guys, cut it out. I've been thinking about the campaign. And I think cupcakes and campaigns have a lot in common. I don't need to crush anyone and I don't need to try to convince anybody of how nice I am." I took the already cooled cupcakes off the cooling rack and placed them on a tray. Using a butter knife, I began to top the yellow cupcakes with my new, super-chocolaty frosting.

"See, to make this new frosting taste better, I switched some ingredients and added my own flavor. I think the campaign is kind of like that. You can look at the way our forefathers did it, but mix it up..."

"...And add our own flavor," Sara said, finishing my sentence.

Lauren mumbled, "And be like George Washington and crush the competition."

"Lauren!" Sara let out a big sigh. "Nobody ran against George Washington. There was no competition!"

Now we were all laughing as we finished frosting the cupcakes that had already cooled. We each chose a cupcake for ourselves. The kitchen was really warm because the oven had been on. Grandpa yanked the sliding glass patio door open and sort of stumbled into the kitchen.

"I smell cupcakes!" he said.

"They are *soooo* good!" Lauren said.

"Well, move over and let Grandpa have a look-see."

We took our cupcakes and glasses of milk onto the patio. We were still licking the frosting off our fingers when...

WHANG!

A noise that loud and unmistakable could mean only one thing:

The band across the back alley was practicing.

"What is that horrible noise?" asked Becks, covering her ears.

"Follow me!" I said.

We ran through my backyard to the gate and pushed it open. The whanging of the guitar got drowned out by the chop-chop-chop-BOOM of the drumsticks.

Across the alley was a garage and inside were four teenage boys playing instruments with one girl singer, Layla Prince, out front.

Layla was like this total **rebel chick**, really cool!

Even though the music was so loud it hurt our ears, we sat crisscross on the grass, pressed our hands to our ears to dull the BOOM and the *whang*, then rocked back and forth.

Layla looked right at us while she sang, and Toby Z. on guitar did a special *whang-whang-whang* thing that I knew was just for us.

When they finished the song, we got to our feet. Toby Z. came out and stood next to Layla.

"What's up?" Toby Z. was cool. He was tall and thin and could drive. He delivered pizzas AND played in a band.

"We were over at Bree's house helping with her campaign," Sara said.

"What we need now," Lauren said, "is a killer slogan. You know, a catchy way for kids to remember that Brianna is the best! Brianna is totally going to be president of the whole fifth grade. We're helping her."

Layla and Toby gave each other high school looks. You know. How teenagers look at each other when they think us elementary school kids are being *sooo* adorable.

Layla said, "That's so adorable!"

See. Told ya.

She stretched and shook her thick, wooly brown hair. It wasn't quite an Afro, but it wasn't exactly straight.

"What's your band's name?" Sara asked.

Layla and the others looked at each other, slow smiles spreading across their faces. Layla said, "Pinks 257."

Lauren asked, "What does that mean?"

Layla shrugged. "Old Lady Pink lives over there," she said, pointing to the white house next to Toby Z.'s yellow house. "Her house number is two-five-seven," Layla added.

Toby scratched his chin where he had a little fuzz growing, sort of like the mold that puffs up on an old orange. "She goes to Bible study from four to six, and because she complains to our folks, that's the only time we can rehearse. So we decided to dedicate our band name to her."

We all cracked up.

"So, you guys are looking for a slogan?" Layla said.

"We were going to make campaign buttons and posters. There's a rally on Friday. We just haven't figured out what it should say," Sara went on.

Lauren said, "It should be catchy."

We all started shouting ideas and giggling because we were saying some goofy stuff, when we heard the drummer count out, "A-one, a-two, a-one, two, three..."

Then he was drumming and Toby Z. was back on the guitar and the keyboard guy was jamming, and Layla took the mike and wailed:

> *She needs your vote; freedom's not free.*
> *She will fight for your lib-er-ty.*
> *This girl is smart, so let's hear it.*
> *Brianna Justice has spirit.*
> *No need to worry, she won't forget; Brianna Justice*
>   *is your best bet!*

So cast your vote—no need to stall.

A vote for Brianna means... Justice for all!

And just like that, we had a slogan.

Who on Earth could top having an almost famous real-life band make up a song just for them? Who could possibly top that?

❀ *Brianna's Cookbook* ❀

Becks told me all the top TV cooks start out with cookbooks. I keep a notebook filled with all my recipes. One day, with Becks's writing help, of course, it'll get published and we'll be superstars!

Chocolate Frosting

2 ³/₄ cups confectioners' sugar
7 tablespoons unsweetened cocoa powder
6 tablespoons butter
4 tablespoons sweetened condensed milk
¹/₂ to 1 cup regular milk
1 teaspoon vanilla extract

1. First, add the dry ingredients in a medium-size bowl; in second bowl, cream the butter with condensed milk.

2. Combine milk-and-butter mixture with dry ingredients, slowly adding in 1/2 to 1 cup of regular milk and vanilla flavoring. You can add more milk to make the frosting creamier or more confectioners' sugar to thicken it up.

3. Now take a bite, but sit down first. This frosting is so good it'll knock you off your feet!

Timeline—American History

1765	1770	1773
Stamp Act Congress meets.	Boston Massacre	Tea Act

1776	1783	1792
Declaration of Independence	American colonies win Revolutionary War against Great Britain.	First U.S. Mint

Timeline—Disaster

4 p.m.	4:30 p.m.	5:30 p.m.
Pinks 257 creates perfect campaign slogan.	I go home for dinner.	Jasmine Moon plays dirty!

7
The First Attack!

While I had been in my backyard with Pinks 257, apparently Jasmine Moon was in the park passing out little triangle-shaped bribes.

Triangles covered in meat and cheese!

Lauren told me she'd heard that Jasmine Moon went to Orchard Park and passed out pizza that same day. Her father bought LOTS of pizza and she was just giving it away to kids "as a way of introducing herself."

Ha!

Should I really believe that? Like people go around saying *Hi, I'm new in town; have some pizza.*

A guilty feeling scratched at the back of my mind.

What if she had only wanted to make friends? What if her pizza was *not* an underhanded way of buying votes?

Besides, hadn't my friends warned me not to get too carried away? She was new. She passed around some pizza. Big deal...right?

Well, what happened next stung more than the time I got flipped in karate class and saw stars.

We three candidates were picking our campaign teams before the big "primary"—which is what they call the little elections in each classroom before the BIG election involving the whole school.

Of course, I'm picking all my girls, right?

With my first pick, I chose Sara. We'd discussed it all through the summer like a gazillion times. She would be my campaign manager. Then Becks. Becks would be in charge of the creative stuff, like slogans and posters. Lauren, who was taller than almost anybody in fifth grade, would be in charge of making sure our posters were hung the best. We had it all planned.

Except, guess what:

Jasmine Moon picked Becks first!

Becks looked all squirmy and nervous.

When Mrs. Nutmeg smiled at Becks, I knew there was trouble. She bent down at Becks's desk, right in front of me. She said, "It might be a nice show of citizenship if you helped our newest student with her election campaign, Sweet Pea."

Mrs. Nutmeg could make going to juvie hall sound like the kindest, greatest thing that could happen to a kid. When she smiled at us and patted us on the back and called us "Sweet Pea," we were putty in her hands. Becks didn't stand a chance!

From the back of the room, Toady Todd began imitating Becks.

"*Umm...mmm...mum...,*" he said, screwing his face up into these real pathetic-looking expressions, then he laughed real hard and in true frog fashion I think he croaked a little. He was the funniest toad he knew.

"Todd Hampton, you will control yourself this instant, or the primary will be over by default, young man, because you will be *out!*" Mrs. Nutmeg glared at him.

Jasmine Moon looked as if she might be nervous. She said, "I'm sorry, Mrs. Nutmeg. I didn't mean to cause any problems. If Rebecca *has* to work with Brianna, I... well, I'm really, really sorry."

45

"Rebecca is free to make her own choices, right, Brianna?" Mrs. Nutmeg looked at me the way Mom does when she's asking something like, *"You do know you're not a grown-up, right, Brianna?"*

Then if that weren't bad enough, Jasmine Moon looked at Becks and said, "It's just that I don't know many people, but you live down the street from me. We could just walk right down the block, you know." From the far side of the room, Taurus the snake slithered around in his glass box. The fish tank made its usual *bloop-bloop-bloop* sounds. The big, black hand on the huge clock over the door seemed to get stuck, just sitting there.

Becks looked at me, then at Sara, as if she didn't know what to do.

Mrs. Nutmeg placed her hand on Becks's shoulder. "I know you have close ties in the class, but maybe just this once…"

Becks gave a small nod.

And just like that, Jasmine Moon had lured one of my best friends…over to the OTHER SIDE!!!

8

"A Chicken in Every Pot!"

Who was I?

No, I hadn't fallen down, hit my head, and lost my memory. I was just asking myself what Mrs. Nutmeg had told all the candidates to think about: She'd said once we understood ourselves—our strengths and weaknesses— it would help us understand what kind of leader we could be and help us come up with good slogans so that the voters could understand us, too.

So I'd been thinking about it since I brushed my teeth that morning. Who was I?

I was Brianna Diane Justice.

I had a mother and a father and a bossy older sister. My dad worked as a nurse and liked restoring old cars.

My mom worked for the FBI—not in the exciting part. She mostly worked on catching people who did crimes on computers. She was a tomboy like me. She taught me to play basketball, ride a bike, and tumble over and over without throwing up.

Dad taught me how to change the oil in the car, how to run a mile without passing out, and how to bake.

I was the reigning champion of our school's penmanship award. I'd won two years in a row.

Let's see...what else?

I planned to be a millionaire chef when I grew up. 'Cause remember, being president of the whole fifth grade is the first step in my lifelong plan to be a successful cupcake chef and millionaire. Without Becks, I settled on this kid named Kenny. I didn't know him too well, but everyone had heard about how good he was in art. A good artist could make some good posters, right?

Mrs. Nutmeg was talking about President Herbert Hoover and his campaign slogan, "A chicken in every pot." She said that slogan was important because around that time the country was in something called the Great Depression. A lot of people didn't have jobs then and were hungry.

So if Hoover was going to guarantee they'd all have chicken, he was the man they'd vote for. I thought about some other facts I'd read about Hoover. He'd made his fortune in gold. Funny, huh? How a man who was popular because he'd gone from being really poor to really rich then became president while most of the country was really poor. Mrs. Nutmeg said he had a hard time helping people get their lives fixed up. I looked at the board, where Mrs. Nutmeg had written another slogan:

"I like Ike" — 1952 U.S. presidential campaign slogan of Dwight D. Eisenhower

"This is an example of a candidate making a play on his own name as a way for voters to remember him," Mrs. Nutmeg said. Just like I was planning to do. *Justice for All*... And with the way things were going, I was going to need some justice, big time.

"But his name is Dwight, right?" asked Todd.

"That's correct," said Mrs. Nutmeg.

"Then who is Ike?" Todd said.

I turned around in my seat. "Ike is his nickname. That's what people called him. *Duh!*"

"Oh, yeah. Like you were there."

"Enough!" Mrs. Nutmeg interjected. "You have one more evening to work on your campaigns. Tomorrow is the in-class campaign primary. Candidates can pass out buttons or posters or goodies. Then Todd, Jasmine, and Brianna will each give a speech and describe three personal traits they possess that would make them a great president."

The bell rang and I was getting my backpack out of my cubby when I felt someone come up behind me. I looked over my shoulder, but I already knew it could only be one person.

Jasmine Moon.

"I had no idea what a wonderful writer your friend Rebecca is. We worked on my speech all day yesterday!"

And before I could say anything, she was gone.

"What?" Sara asked when she and Lauren came over and saw me looking as if I'd just swallowed a spider.

"I think she did it on purpose!" I whispered. "She picked Becks because she knows good and well that Becks is the best writer in the whole fifth grade!"

Sara looked skeptical. "But how could she know that?

She's only been here like two minutes. It was just lucky for her, that's all."

As we were leaving class, I thought about it. Maybe Sara was right. Maybe it was just Jasmine Moon's good luck.

But I couldn't shake the feeling. Was Jasmine Moon just a lucky girl who happened to wind up with my best friend on her campaign team and gave out pizza just to introduce herself?

Or was she some sort of political evil genius?

Did you know there was a president named Theodore "Teddy" Roosevelt, and he's the one they named the teddy bear after? Well, there was and they did.

All I can think about now is how cool it would be to have people buy cupcakes named after me!!!

My big, secret, super-spectacular idea for the campaign came from something Mrs. Nutmeg wrote on the board: the Boston Tea Party and the creation of the first U.S. Mint.

And that gave me an idea. Here are a few things I'll need for tomorrow:

- An inflatable kiddie pool

- Chocolates

- Tea bags

9
A Spy!

After school, I stopped Becks in the hall. Lauren and Sara were always the last to leave class because they helped Mrs. Nutmeg clean the animal cages and take care of the small zoo we had in there, including a brown ferret, a green snake, a large fish tank, and Bubba the overweight turtle.

"Becks, don't feel bad; it's not your fault."

She blew out another long sigh, as if she'd been holding her breath again. "I just don't want to hurt anybody's feelings," she said.

Now it was my turn to take a big gulp of air. I had thought of another idea. One that I thought would make everything work for everybody.

"Becks, I was wondering, what if, while you're helping her, you tell me what she's up to."

"You mean SPY?!!" Becks's eyes were rounder than a full moon, and she looked guiltier than a kid covered in cookie crumbs before dinner.

"*Shhhh!*" I snapped. I pulled her to one side of the hall hoping they couldn't hear us all the way downstairs in the principal's office. All I needed was to get a black mark on my permanent record in fifth grade. How would I start my cupcake empire if I couldn't get into college, go to business school, start my own business, and launch an empire using the valuable leadership skills I learned as president of my whole fifth-grade class? Becks helped me write most of that this summer, part of my acceptance speech. Anyway, how would I do any of that if my permanent record got jacked up for spying on the competition?

"Remember in class today? Mrs. Nutmeg told us about some general guy, Thomas Cage or Gage, something like that." The general was a British commander in Boston and he knew that someone close to him was spying on his army.

Becks nodded. "Mrs. Nutmeg said they never figured out who it was, but they thought it was his wife!"

"Exactly. I mean, you wouldn't have to do anything creepy. Just, you know, sort of let me know what's going on. You know, in case I need to make my campaign better. Just think, you'll still be helping me, just like we planned all summer. Except now you can help in a different way. Will you do it?"

Becks's dark eyes turned stormy and her bushy brown brows squished together. I knew that look. That was her "uh-oh" face. As in, "Uh-oh, something awful is about to happen." She frowned and bit her lip. She looked at the ground and dug around in her book bag for her inhaler.

"Just think about it," I said. "It could be a secret, just between you and me. Okay?"

The door to the classroom opened. Sara and Lauren had finished and were heading to the restroom to wash their hands.

"Meet you guys downstairs at the bike racks," I said.

But when I turned around to loop my arm around Becks, something silly we did sometimes when we were walking together, I let out a tiny gasp.

Jasmine Moon had beat me to it.

"I thought you could come over to my house today," she said, her voice honey-sweet. Honest to goodness, she had her arm looped into Becks's just like I always did.

Had she already been spying on us? On me?

Becks looked like one of my sister Katy's rescued stray cats after I'd trapped it under a laundry basket. Whenever I did it, I'd yell for Katy to come and spring her animal from kitty jail.

Becks looked like she was in kitty jail. Poor Becks.

I gave a small nod toward Becks, to remind her what we'd talked about. Later, as I rode my bike along with Lauren and Sara, I didn't mention my plan. Was I going overboard? Getting too crazy? Sara would probably roll her eyes and sigh and tell me to back off. Lauren might push Becks too hard, get her all nervous, and ruin everything.

Or maybe I didn't mention it because, well, I couldn't believe I asked my best friend to sneak around and get information. For me!

The thought of Becks spying gave me a tiny shiver along my spine, cold like rain down your collar. Icy cold, like secrets . . . or *fear.*

ELECTION NOTEBOOK

- An Act—during the American Revolution, the people of Great Britain came up with laws or "acts" for the new Americans to obey.

- Colonists—people who came from Great Britain to form the New World (which is what they called America).

- All of these Acts were like laws, and if the Americans didn't follow them they'd get in big trouble. Which is really stupid when you think about it because the king should have known if you send people far, far away and call them the New World, then they don't want to still act like **the *Old* World.**

- So of course the New World people didn't want to put up with the Sugar Act (1764) that made it cost more for sugar and other stuff.

- The Quartering Act (1765) said colonists had to provide a place to stay for up to 10,000 British troops. (Who wants 10,000 British army men in their house tracking in mud and eating their food?)

- Since tea back then was as popular as soda or chocolate milk today, **the Tea Act** (1773), which said colonists could buy tea only from Britain's East India Company, made the **New Worlders** go bananas.

- So the colonists got mad and dressed up like Mohawk warriors and sneaked on a ship and dumped 342 chests of tea into the Boston Harbor.

10

Intolerable Acts of the Fifth Grade

The next morning I was up before the alarm went off. It was Friday. All the candidates and their campaign teams were meeting at school early to hang signs and plan strategy. I felt excited and jittery and sort of weird all at the same time.

Pig Pig gave me an encouraging wink. I made sure my ponytails were extra fluffy. I chose my money-clip barrettes for extra good luck!

I'd met with Lauren, Sara, and Kenny after school yesterday. We'd blown up balloons, gone over my speech, made more posters, and arranged cupcakes in plastic containers. All the while, I couldn't help thinking about Becks.

Would she spy on Jasmine Moon for me?

Would she tell me if Jasmine Moon was planning some really spectacular presentation that might just blow me out of the election?

Was it cheating to ask Becks to pass along information?

Downstairs I made myself some French toast, careful to keep an eye on the stove. Technically, my parents didn't want me messing around in the kitchen when they weren't up, but as long as I didn't start any fires, I figured they wouldn't really mind.

Besides, French toast was so easy. I took a few egg yolks, whisked them together, and added a bit of milk, cinnamon, and a teaspoon of vanilla flavoring. Then, I heated our skillet with some sweet butter, dipped a few slices of thick bread into the egg mixture, and plopped it into the hot skillet.

The coffeepot was perking up while the toast was cooking.

"Smells amazing in here!"

I almost jumped out of my shoes.

"Dad! You scared me. Want some?"

"Sure."

So I shared my French toast and had my coffee. I'm only allowed a half cup on school days and a whole cup on the weekend. Dad handed me the business section of the paper while he went straight to the sports section. Warm French toast and coffee in my tummy, my lucky barrettes and my ponytails extra fluffy—it was time to get this party started.

After I got to school and we hung up our posters, we all wondered where Becks and Jasmine Moon were. We finished by the time the first bell rang.

With two minutes till the second bell, in walked Tabitha Handy, Robin Geller, Jasmine Moon, and Rebecca.

"So, what's up?" I said. Becks took her seat in front of me. She dumped her hefty backpack on the floor and took out her notebook and favorite pencil box. She set her inhaler on the right side of her desk, easy to get to if she needed it later.

"Guess what?" she said when she spun around.

"Settle down, fifth graders; we have much to do today. I need your full attention," Mrs. Nutmeg said.

Becks covered her mouth with her hand and whispered, "Everything's going to be okay. Jasmine Moon is really nice. She doesn't think she can win. She just wants to make friends. You'll see. You don't have anything to worry about."

For the next hour Mrs. Nutmeg led us through our vocabulary assignment, then we started math. I could barely concentrate. All I could think about was what Becks had said about Jasmine Moon.

"She just wants to make friends."

By the time lunch rolled around, I was itching to get to the cafeteria. I needed to know what was going on with Becks and what else she would tell me.

"Class, I have a surprise for you."

Mrs. Nutmeg told us that instead of the cafeteria, she'd arranged for us to have lunch in our classroom. She'd ordered pizza!

"Now we can use the time we have until the pizza arrives to talk about the election."

Everyone else was all excited. Toady and his tadpoles were saying "Yeah!" and high-fiving each other. Surprise pizza parties sort of had that effect on kids. Can't explain it. Just a fact of fifth-grade life.

Mrs. Nutmeg was talking again, this time about past presidents and some of their personal traits. It was hard to concentrate, though, because the whole time I kept wanting Becks to look around. But she never did.

"Voters need to trust a candidate. So it's important to know not only how the candidates stand on the issues, but also who they are and how they act."

At first, I thought I was going to explode. I was trying so hard to make the time pass faster, but then I actually got to listening to Mrs. Nutmeg, and all of a sudden I didn't want her to stop. With a competition on presidential trivia for the kids who win the primary, learning as many facts as possible was necessary. And Mrs. Nutmeg was cramming so many facts in our brains I thought my head would burst.

Like, I'd never heard that President George Washington liked to put out fires. He was a volunteer firefighter.

Or that John Quincy Adams was the first president to be photographed.

And **Thomas Jefferson** kept a mockingbird named "Dick" in the White House and let it ride around on his shoulder. How cool was that?

When the pizza arrived, a lot of us didn't want Mrs. Nutmeg to stop. I volunteered to help pass out the pizza and napkins. Becks looked up as I handed her a slice of pizza. She took it and said, "Don't worry about the speech. Even though I helped her, I know yours will be awesome. But could you promise me one thing?"

"What?" I asked.

"Don't be mad." Becks's expression went from all happy and smiley to squirmy and nervous.

I pretended to drop a napkin and then bent down to pick it up so I could whisper in her ear. "Mad about what?"

"I . . . just don't want to hurt your feelings, but maybe she's really like us."

"Really? Jasmine Moon?"

Before she could answer, Miss Moon herself came up and put her arm around Becks's shoulder.

"Rebecca," she sang out. I rolled my eyes. "Hey, Brianna, good luck today." Jasmine Moon shook her crinkly hair at me. She was really starting to get on my nerves. Was I being too sensitive?

And then—here's the worst part ever—Becks gave me her "It'll all work out" look and I knew, knew right then that Jasmine Moon had gotten inside her head. Oh, Becks! How can you be so blind?

"Rebecca was so much help. She talked about you *all*

day. Told me a lot about you. Well, good luck today. Really. I'm sure you'll do awesome," said Jasmine Moon.

What had Becks told her about me?

My stomach churned. I didn't want to admit it, but I felt ashamed that I'd asked Becks to spy. And scared, too. Was it possible that Becks told Jasmine Moon that I wanted her to spy?

11

The Race Is On

"We should call them Moon Bots," said Lauren as we watched Jasmine Moon and her posse hang all over each other and go around the room spreading their **foolishness,** one student at a time.

It was time for the candidates to start introducing ourselves before we did our speeches. I knew everybody in the room, but it was kinda fun and kinda funny to shake their hands, and mostly everybody just laughed and it was nice.

An hour before the final bell, we'd talked to all the kids in the class and passed out cupcakes to everyone.

"Brianna, your cupcakes are so, so, *sooooo* good!" said Nancy Chen.

Even Mrs. Nutmeg ate a cupcake. "Very tasty, Brianna," she said. I felt a warm, happy feeling in my belly. Over summer break, I was at a party store with my dad getting stuff for a July Fourth picnic. That's when I spotted these little plastic dollar signs that stick right up in a cake or cupcake. I used my whole allowance that week to buy them and put them aside because I knew I'd want to use them for the election when school started. They were red, white, and blue and sparkled. *Perfect for a school election!*

I'd read on the Internet that a successful political campaign relied on the candidate really getting her message to the people.

Well, my message was simple: I'm a great cupcake maker. I want to make cupcakes and millions when I grow up.

And I want *Justice for All!*

Even when there used to be a president in each fifth-grade class, those kids were in charge of a class budget. They were in charge of holding sales, working with their teachers on charity fund-raisers, and raising money for class trips and projects. So letting the kids know I was a girl who could handle her money was *really* important.

Kenny drew a huge dollar bill, but instead of George Washington he had drawn a cupcake in the center. He'd written "The U.S. Mint" around the cupcake, and on the bottom he'd written "Justice Dollars."

I had my own money! Isn't that the first real step to world domination?

Everybody who took a cupcake also got a piece of green construction paper that Sara and Lauren had worked on. They'd cut them the size of dollar bills and drawn lines and everything so it would sort of look like money; only each piece had cupcakes in the center just like Kenny's big poster, and the same words. In each corner it said "Brianna Justice."

Todd shouldered a cupcake-eating voter out of the way.

I glared at Toady. He snatched up two cupcakes and shoved them in his mouth. Then Mrs. Nutmeg said it was time to do our presentations and the first name she called was Todd Hampton. He still had cupcake frosting stuck to his face and the side of his mouth when he went to the front of the class.

"My name is Todd T. Hampton." *Yeah, the "T" is for*

Toad, I thought. He went on. "Here is why you should vote for me."

I held my breath. The whole class went silent. All eyes were on Todd.

Deep, deep, deep down in my stomach, I could feel myself getting all clenched up like the way your toes curl at a scary movie. What if he was really good? What if everybody liked him better than me? What if he said mean things about me and everybody laughed?

"I know you all know me...," Todd began. Then something really weird happened. I noticed the paper he was holding was sort of shaking.

That's when I knew: Toady Todd Hampton was nervous.

He cleared his throat and tried to laugh. "Go on, Mr. Hampton," Mrs. Nutmeg said.

"Give me a minute, will ya?" he said.

Then...nothing. He just stood up there and looked at us.

"Todd?" Mrs. Nutmeg said again.

Then he got real huffy and said, "All right, all right. I just want to say, here are some things to know about me.

First, I like hockey. Number two, I'm the tallest one in the class. And last, um, well, just vote for me 'cause I'm the best."

Then he balled up the paper and walked really fast back to his seat.

I couldn't help looking back at him. He slumped down in his seat and a few of the tadpoles started pointing and laughing at him. He didn't even tell them to shut up or anything.

Freaky, right? I almost felt sorry for him.

"Very well, Todd. Next we'll have..."

My heart was doing double Dutch. All I could think was, *Please don't say my name. Please don't say my name. Please don't say my name!*

"...Jasmine Moon. Would you come up and present your speech to the class."

I let out a big exhale. I really wanted to go last. I needed to know if my presentation was as good as the competition's.

"Don't be mad, okay?" Becks whispered.

Her voice made me jump.

Then she got up and went to the coat closet and got a long black case, and then she went and stood next to

Jasmine Moon. She opened the case and took out her flute.

Jasmine started her speech, and Becks began playing the flute. It was just like some old war movie you might catch your dad taking a nap in front of on a Saturday afternoon.

And if that wasn't bad enough, another boy I'd known since pre-K strapped a drum around his neck, stood up there with them, and played; and it was all very much like a school play.

And Jasmine Moon was the star!

"Students of Room three-eighteen, we are fifth graders. Before I tell you about myself, I just want to say it would be my honor to be your class representative in the elections. When George Washington became president, people elected him not because they'd known him his whole life; not because he thought he was *supposed* to be president; but because he was the best person for the job."

I couldn't stop looking at Becks. Did she come up with all that stuff? Were they talking about me? Like I thought I was all that and that everybody should vote for me just because?

I mean, I wasn't anything like that! Right? RIGHT???

"What traits do I have that would make me a great president of the fifth grade? I am a good student. I've been a Girl Scout since first grade and I believe in helping others. And just like Thomas Jefferson, I play the violin."

Hmph! Thomas Jefferson did a lot more than play the violin. Did you know he came up with the idea to base America's money system around decimals, using 100 cents as the base? See, Jefferson knew we needed an easy way to count our money. I like counting money. So, hey, I had as much in common with good ol' T.J. as Jasmine Moon did!

She kept talking, and as soon as she said "Thank you," the entire class was applauding and grinning. This time when I looked at Becks, she looked as if she was lost somewhere between jumping with joy and bursting into tears. Maybe she just needed her inhaler after all that flute playing.

Sara said to Becks, "Glad to see all those flute lessons your mom made you take are paying off!" Becks bit her lip and rushed to her desk, where she took two big puffs from her inhaler. She spun around quickly, and before I could say a word, she started:

"See. Don't be mad. It was really good, right? But who cares, because we all know you're the best and you're totally going to win and Jasmine is okay with that and I just—"

"Now if we could have Miss Brianna Justice to the front of the room," Mrs. Nutmeg cut in. She was standing right at Becks's desk with her arms crossed. I was beginning to think I had the world's loudest spy!

Lauren was already on her feet heading toward the front of the room, while Jasmine made her way back to her seat.

"Mrs. Nutmeg, we're going to need the computer to help with Bree's speech," Lauren said.

"Class, our third and final candidate, Miss Brianna Justice."

My stomach burned, and for about a second I feared that leftover Crest from brushing my teeth that morning would come shooting out of my nose. Not to mention the French toast. *Urp!*

I took a deep breath, then blew it out. It was like being

at the free-throw line with the score tied at the end of the game. My knees trembled. Then I remembered how I'd made free throws "my thing." How hard I'd worked to become the best free-throw shooter on the team.

"My name is Brianna Justice, and I want to be your president." Soon as I said the words, it was like hitting the first shot of my one-and-one. The trembling stopped, but I went on. "I have many traits that might help me be a great president, but here are a few things I'll share with you today. First, I love basketball. I love to play and I love to watch. The Pistons are my favorite professional team. Michigan State is my favorite college team."

Now the kids were sitting up, paying attention, and I didn't feel as nervous.

"Another thing you probably know about me is that I love to bake."

Almost the entire class, all at the same time, said: "We know, we know..."

Then the quietest kid in the class said, "You're going to be a famous cupcake maker with your own TV show and make lots of money."

My face got really, really hot. Should I run screaming from the room? Jump out the window?

Wait a minute!

They were all smiling.

Everybody.

Were my eyes playing tricks on me, or were the Back Row Boys—Toady Todd included—also smiling?

I let out a long breath and smiled, too. "Okay, so maybe I've mentioned it once or twice."

More laughter. Hey, this speech thing was going pretty well.

Kenny had poured water into the inflatable pool, and Lauren pressed play on the DVD player. Layla's voice sang from the computer speakers and the image of Pinks 257 filled the monitor.

Lauren, Sara, and Kenny all sang along:

She needs your; vote; freedom's not free.
She will fight for your lib-er-ty.

We passed out sheets of paper that had all the words on it, and we were telling the others to sing along.

When it got to the next part, more people sang with us.

> *This girl is smart, so let's hear it.*
> *Bri-anna Justice has spirit.*
> *No need to worry, she won't forget; Brianna Justice*
> *is your best bet!*

Now most of the kids were bobbing their heads and singing along.

> *So cast your vote — no need to stall.*
> *A vote for Brianna means...*
> *Justice for all! Justice for all! Justice for all! Justice*
> *for all!*

We opened small boxes while each of us walked down the rows passing out tea bags. We had everybody stand and form a line, walking up to the pool and throwing in their tea bags. You know, like the Americans did to protest all those high taxes back in the 1700s. We weren't protesting anything, but I knew everyone would get a kick out of slamming those tea bags into the pool and watching the water go from clear to all-American mud color.

It was way, way cool.

By the time it ended, the entire class, including Toady Todd Hampton and his crew, were standing and singing and nobody was looking at Jasmine Moon.

It was the perfect way to end the day. I went home feeling unbeatable. Everything was perfect, *until*...

12

*Un*common Sense!

Have you ever felt blue?

You know. Weird. Down in the dumps. Blue. And you couldn't quite figure out why.

That's how I felt on Saturday.

The day started well enough. I got up, read the morning paper, and sipped my cup of coffee. It was Saturday, so I had a full cup and added French vanilla cream and a dab of whipped cream. So, so good.

I flipped through the sales papers, didn't see anything great, then went straight for Aunt Tina's column. Every Saturday she had a column that ran on the front of the business section. The columns almost always highlighted some new product or invention or told the story of a person from the area who'd taken their small business dream and made it a reality.

I loved those columns the most!

Today's column, though, was about a man whose business had failed. He talked about how he'd put everything he had into it, but he was so focused on his product, he said, that he'd forgotten to do what it took to run a successful business. I thought about that. This guy offered a good product—New York–style pizza—but the column says he went out of business because he didn't take care of those who helped him. His staff. His peeps.

That would never happen to me, I vowed. I was going to focus on my product—cupcakes—*and* my peeps.

After a while, like every Saturday, Sara's mom picked me up for our weekly "Woodhull Society Saturday" trips to make deposits. Then we got Lauren and Becks and went to the bank. We'd all had savings accounts for a long time.

Like always, inside the bank the four of us walked to the bank teller together.

"Morning, girls," said Mrs. Sanchez. When she smiled, a tiny dimple showed in her cheek. We like

Mrs. Sanchez. We'd gotten to know her over the years of saving here.

"Good morning, Mrs. Sanchez," I said.

"*Cómo está?*" said Sara.

We all gave her a look. She shrugged and said, "What? I've been practicing my Spanish."

"*Muy bien, gracias!*" Mrs. Sanchez responded. We passed her our deposit slips. We'd each written our very own account numbers on our slips. My deposit was twenty-six dollars—ten dollars for allowance; ten dollars for helping Mr. Kruger down the block rake up all the grass and gunk in his yard after he mowed his lawn. The other six dollars came from Katy. She was always borrowing money!

After our deposits, we sat in Mrs. Parker's car with the motor running and ancient music from the eighties blaring from the car stereo. Sara turned deep red and said, "Mom, please!" as her mom snapped her fingers and started singing along to a song she said was a big hit when she was in college.

We tried not to laugh. Sara's mom had a little bit of an accent and it made the bad singing sound even funnier.

Sara looked like she wanted to hide in the air vent. (Still, it was kind of funny!)

We were waiting for my aunt Tina. Sometimes she'd pick us up either here or at the Parkers' and take us to breakfast on Saturdays. Her treat, she said, to further the cause of "sisters who're doing it for themselves!" Aunt Tina was great.

Anyway, the blueness sort of kicked in while we were waiting. Usually, a trip to deposit my ten-dollar-a-week allowance left me feeling excited, filled with plans on what it would be like to own my own business. How I'd be able to help my dad get that new car he's always wanted. I'd even donate generously to Katy's homeless animal shelter that she wanted to run someday!

Thanks to saving all of my birthday and Christmas gifts for as long as I could remember, plus earning cash for doing extra chores at home and around the neighborhood over the summer, I had over 500 dollars in the bank! The four of us had already planned how, in a few weeks, when the leaves started falling, we would rake leaves together around our neighborhoods and earn even more money.

Whenever I thought about all that money, I got a little giddy. One day I'd use it to bake the greatest cupcakes and desserts in the world!

But instead of feeling strong, powerful, and green with cash, I was blue.

One reason: I couldn't stop thinking about the man in Aunt Tina's column. Grandpa would call that "not being able to see the forest for the trees," which I think meant somebody was so busy looking at the big thing, they didn't pay attention to the little things.

Was I forgetting to take care of the little things?

What were my "little things"? I groaned. I was definitely getting a headache, worrying about my friends, my goals, my business, and being president of the whole fifth grade.

But that wasn't the only reason my head was starting to pound. Becks had a lot to do with it, too!

The whole time we waited for Aunt Tina to roll up in her car, Becks was going on and on about Jasmine Moon.

"She's so nice, you guys. She really wants to get to know all of us and hang out..."

And...

"I told her about how we're all saving our money to be millionaires..." and then "Jasmine is sooooo smart and she has a lot of cute clothes..." and then "Jasmine Moon's dad works for the Pistons and she said he'd get us tickets to the games...."

She just wouldn't stop talking.

And the way she went on and on about every little Jasmine Moon detail was really starting to bug me.

Not once did she say one thing about my speech on Friday. And she didn't say *anything* about our agreement. She was supposed to be spying for me, not the other way around.

Once we got to the restaurant, a diner downtown called Lou's, we got our usual table. Even Aunt Tina noticed how Becks wouldn't shut up about Jasmine Moon. But instead of telling her to chill, she said, "Sounds like that girl made quite an impression on you, Miss B."

Becks nodded, saying, "I just know that no matter what happens in the election, she'll want to be our friend."

No matter what happens in the election? *What?*

"Well, she sounds lovely, but if you think she'd be

any match against Brianna over here, well, that's foolishness!" When she said "foolishness," she sang it out like opera.

"You are so much like your aunt," Lauren whispered.

"Baby Girl is smart and a natural-born leader. I know she'll make an excellent president." Aunt Tina had been calling me "Baby Girl," well, since I was a baby.

We all clinked our glasses together, and I was starting to feel a little better, until . . . Aunt Tina added:

"Just make sure you find a way to make yourself stand out. You've got to make sure the voters see you as an individual. Someone they can remember. The one thing that new girl has over you is mystery. People might be intrigued by her because they *don't* know her. She might seem somehow mystical. For someone like you, someone who's been there, the trick is to be bold. Be daring!"

By the time breakfast ended and we were all dropped at our homes, all I could think about was Aunt Tina and what she'd said.

"Be daring!"

What she said was something I'd already been thinking—and worrying—about.

Kids were intrigued by Jasmine Moon and her extra-crinkly black hair. She was a little mysterious. And that made her seem more interesting. Why vote for boring Brianna whom they'd known since forever when they could vote for **Mystery**?

But the true blueness began when later Saturday afternoon, Katy and I both got yelled at by Mom after we got to yelling at each other because I called her Queen of the Litter Box and then she said, "Don't count your votes too soon. It takes more than a catchy slogan to win a campaign. It sounds like this Jasmine girl is going to be tough to beat."

Anyway, like I said, we got yelled at for "acting like brats" and told to "clean up those dirty bedrooms." *Hmph!* Okay, so my headquarters—that's what I called my bedroom—were a little crusty.

Hey, when a girl is planning to take over the world one cupcake recipe at a time, she can forget about the little things.

For the next few hours I scooped laundry, changed bed linens, folded or hung up clothes, and stacked magazines and books in their proper places.

I even dusted the huge poster of Miss Delicious that hung above my desk while I watched her show on television. Her TV kitchen was filled with pinks and reds with little touches of black here and there. Miss Delicious was talking about adding coffee to chocolate as I folded the last of my clean laundry. She was saying, "Coffee draws out the flavor of chocolate. It enhances it so you and your guests can delight in every little bite!"

Could I add coffee to one of my cupcake recipes? Maybe my chocolate frosting? *Hmm...*

Anyway, right as I was dusting off Pig Pig, our parents announced they were going out to watch Michigan State football with some friends. As soon as they were gone, Katy made her move.

"Shhh," she whispered. "I'm putting a blue streak in one part of my hair. If you tell Mom and Dad before it's done, I'll kill you."

Yeah, yeah, yeah. She was always threatening to kill me; like I even believed that. But I kept my mouth shut. Goody-goody Katy didn't often do things that were considered "wrong." Or "dangerous." I thought it was cool.

We went into her bathroom and she showed me the bottle. We read the instructions. She wet her hair and we squirted the blue goop into her hand. I said, "You should make the stripe bigger."

She said, "No!"

When it was time to rinse it out, I said, "You should leave it in longer, just to be sure."

She said, "No!"

When she finished, she had a blue stripe that was almost as dark as her black hair.

"Told ya!" I said.

"Look, Squirt, I didn't want it to blaze. It's okay, right?"

Then she told me to promise once again not to say anything.

"Katy, why'd you do it if you don't want Mom and Dad to know? You know they're going to find out, right?"

"Oh, I know. It's not permanent. They'll probably have a cow, but, hey, I'm a freshman in high school. I'm in the orchestra. I rescue abandoned pets and volunteer in an animal shelter. None of which puts me in the 'most popular babe' category. Every once in a while I need to do something to let everybody know I'm not just some geeky honors student, you know."

A thought struck me with such force it was like ol' Ben Franklin outside with his kite in the lightning. **ZING!**

Katy wanted to be daring.

Maybe Katy and I had more in common than I thought. I nodded.

Then she said, "Don't you get tired of people thinking they know everything about you? It's so, so...predictable. Every once in a while, I like to shake things up!"

Once Katy dried her hair, she got ready to go to the movies with her friends. I was supposed to go across the street to Grandpa's house, but I told a little fib.

"Grandpa, Katy's not leaving for another hour. Soon as she does, I'll be over," I said.

"Don't dally, gal. I've already picked out some movies on that there rental station on the cable TV. Soon as you make it over, we'll start watching our shows."

I told him I'd hurry.

But first I had a plan.

I ☆ I ☆ I ☆ I

I raced upstairs to Katy's bathroom and removed the half-empty bottle of Skyrocket Blue gel dye from her shower. Then I went into my shower and went to work. I was going to be bold. I was going to be daring. I was going to be the New Brianna!!!

Forty-five minutes later...man, oh, man, I missed the old Brianna.

Because New Brianna...her butt was in so much trouble.

13

Teddy Roosevelt, First President to Fly in Airplane
(Wish I were flying somewhere with him today!)

"I don't care what you say, young lady. You're going to school today, blue hair and all. Maybe that'll teach you a lesson."

Katy cut her eyes at me in the backseat. "Serves you right!" she whispered. "Now I'm grounded for a week because you couldn't mind your own business. *Again*."

I whispered, "It's your fault."

"How is it my fault?"

"You said this stuff washes out."

"It washes out eventually. Like after a month or so. Not the next day."

"But that's not what you said!"

"Stop it! Both of you are in enough trouble!"

"Mom, please! It wasn't supposed to get this blue."

"You should have thought of that..."

My mother continued her lecture and I tried to get lost between the car seat cushions like an *un*lucky penny.

She pulled to the drop-off loop. *"Mommmmmm,"* I pleaded.

"Get out, Squirt. She's going to be late dropping me off." Katy gave me a shove. I looked at her with her blue streak tucked under her black hair. She was right. If it weren't for my bright, fat, wide streak of blue hair, Mom and Dad probably wouldn't have even noticed hers.

Mom wouldn't even look at me. She was furious. I slumped out of the car, my head hung low. I really didn't like it when Mom got mad at me.

For just a brief moment, I thought maybe no one would notice. I'd tried to do it better than Katy had, but when I put that goop in my hair it just spread like blue lava.

Now, instead of two shiny black ponytails touching my shoulders, today fat stripes of dark blue rippled through. I slid out of the car, my shoulders hunched. Then, before I could close the door...

"Hey, Brianna, did you dye your hair blue?"

So much for nobody noticing.

By the time I made it to the third floor and Mrs. Nutmeg opened the door to Room 318, I was already tired of trying to explain why I had blue hair.

First, I'd tried to tell the truth. I'd tried to say it was sort of an accident. My sister's fault.

But everybody kept crowding around. They wanted to touch it, as if blue hair felt different than regular hair.

"Ladies and gentlemen, you don't want me to get to writing names on the board. So get-to-getting!" said Mrs. Nutmeg, her hand on her hip and her eyebrow pointed upward as she eyed my blue streaks with suspicion. Did she think they were contagious? Like if I touched someone in class by the end of the day the whole class would have a horrible case of blue streaks?

I sat in my seat. Todd kicked my chair and said, "Greetings, freak!"

And I caught Jasmine looking at me as if I might blow up or something.

"Class, let me have your attention. Young ladies and

young men, I was proud of all the presentations Friday, but as you know we can have only two representatives per classroom."

My head dropped to my desk. I felt a reassuring hand stroking my back and knew it belonged to Sara.

"...And the two students who will represent us in the class elections are..."

I closed my eyes. I tried to count to ten.

"Jasmine Moon!" When Mrs. Nutmeg announced Jasmine's name, my heart crashed into my throat, then took a dive right into my belly.

"...And..."

Now everybody was looking around the room. I swear, I stopped breathing all together. I was concentrating so hard on trying to breathe that I didn't hear what Mrs. Nutmeg said next.

"You did it!" Sara said, jumping out of her seat to hug me.

I looked up and saw the whole class looking at me. And most everybody was applauding.

I did it. I was an official candidate for fifth-grade president and president of the whole school.

I ☆ I ☆ I ☆ I

Five minutes later . . .

We were called down to Principal Beelie's office. He wanted us to appear on school TV so he could introduce the candidates to the whole school.

Jasmine Moon, with her crinkly dark hair, was on one side and a girl with two long red braids was on the other side. And I was in the middle. Me and my **BLUE, BLUE** hair.

There were ten of us in all, our faces staring into the camera, me wishing I could magically make my blue hair disappear, as Principal Beelie announced:

"Students of Orchard Park Elementary, allow me to introduce to you the student representatives — your candidates for president!"

We had gone to the front office to be introduced during morning announcements. That meant every class was watching. Every student could see us. See me.

And my hair.

I'd have to do some research the way Mrs. Goth in

the media center taught us to see if any of our founding fathers had funny blue hair.

Just when I thought it couldn't get worse, Dr. Beelie placed his hand on my shoulder and frowned, looking as though he'd swallowed an onion, and said, "Young lady, I don't know if we're ready for a president of the fifth grade who has blue hair!"

I groaned. This was my life goal, people. If I didn't become president of the whole fifth grade, could I ever run my own company, bake cupcakes, and become a millionaire?

14

Ask Not What the Fifth Grade Can Do for You...but What You Can Do for a (Certain Sneaky, Creepy, Weaselly) Fifth Grader!

After several days of washing my hair in the shower every night, the blue streak became less noticeable. Kids at school found other things to gossip about. Life went pretty much back to normal.

Except for all the stuff that was going on with the election.

And what *wasn't* going on with me and Becks.

FIVE WEEKS TILL ELECTIONS! Did I mention that I was freaking out?

Becks was still hanging out with Jasmine, "helping" with her campaign. But she hadn't given me one eensy-teensy bit of inside information.

What kind of spy was she, anyway?

I had all sorts of stuff on my mind when I crashed right into the most wily rodent in all of elementary school: Raymond Wetzel, otherwise known as Weasel.

"Good day, m'lady!" When Weasel talked, you couldn't help feeling like he was a villain in some old cartoon. If Weasel were a cartoon drawing, he'd have a long, pointy tail and a skinny mustache.

"What do you want?"

A few kids looked our way, but no one said anything. Weasel was well known for his practical jokes and odd behavior.

"I have something you ought to take a look at," said Weasel.

Typical Weasel. His eyes slid back and forth like he expected the Secret Service, the guys who guard the real president, to come racing around the corner.

"Weasel, get lost. You're not even in our class. I've got to get my bike to ride home." Sara and Lauren were helping with the class pets, as usual. And as usual, at least "usual" for lately, Becks had left with Jasmine Moon and some of her new posse.

I tried pushing past him, but Weasel shoved something into my hand.

An envelope?

I looked at it, frowned, then looked at him.

Weasel had flat, dark eyes and hair the color of dirty pennies. He was always squinting as if the sun was in his eyes even when we were inside the school.

And he was always lurking around.

Everybody believed that's why all his clothes were brown, black, or gray. It's easier to skulk around when you're dressed like a shadow.

"M'lady, it is a matter most urgent!"

"Stop calling me 'm'lady.' And STOP BREATHING ON ME!"

He leaned closer. "*Shhh!* Be warned, m'lady! We must discuss this immediately. It's about the election."

"What about the election?"

"You, dear lady, have a Benedict Arnold in your midst. And if you don't take action immediately, the presidency will be lost!"

ELECTION NOTEBOOK

- In the 1960s, this young guy named John F. Kennedy was president.

- He said, "Ask not what your country can do for you; ask what you can do for your country."

- If he were alive, President Kennedy would want me to figure out not what being president of the whole fifth grade could do for me, but what I could do for the fifth grade!

- I was going to be a good leader; a voice for The People. Just as soon as Becks stopped acting like everything Jasmine Moon said was a poem and started spying for me like she was supposed to!

15

The Real Benedict Arnold!

I led Weasel back to Mrs. Nutmeg's room. That quote she'd written on the bulletin board said it all:

"I have learned to hate all traitors, and there is no disease that I spit on more than treachery." —Aeschylus

Someone I trusted was being a traitor. And that was a betrayal of the highest order!

The room was empty. Sara and Lauren must have left through Mr. Ketterman's classroom.

Weasel's cheeks puffed out with air, then he let out a great sigh.

"Bree, Bree, Bree..."

"WEASEL! Quit it! Only my friends call me 'Bree.' Now, seriously, what do you want?"

Weasel's face fell into a pout. He said, "But I am your friend."

He looked so pitiful when he said it. I felt kind of bad. I'd known the kid since pre-K when he conked me on the head with his rubber sword because he thought he was a knight and I was his princess.

I sighed again. "Okay, you're...sort of my friend. What do you want?"

Weasel smiled his slick smile and bowed like some olden-days dude in tights. Just go along with it, I told myself. He's been like this since he was in diapers.

He said, "M'lady, first allow me to compliment your lovely blue hair. Very daring. Now, if you please, look inside the envelope."

I'd gotten so irritated that I'd forgotten about the envelope. I ripped it open. My heartbeat gave me a karate kick in the chest as I read what was inside.

I took Audrey Murphy's ten-dollar bill. Now Todd is in trouble. I put the money

back when nobody could see me, but Mrs.
Wellaver said it was Todds falt. Shood I tell?
Circle yes or no.   —Brianna

"Where'd you get this?" I felt like somebody was letting the air of me.

Weasel's shadowy face looked grim.

"Dear, sweet, Bree...um, I mean, Miss Justice. This
came from a secret source I have inside the Jasmine
Moon camp. M'lady, they mean you no good."

A photocopy of the old, crinkly paper shook in my
hand. A copy of the original, which only one person in
the whole universe had—REBECCA.

Weasel spoke in a quiet, secretive voice. "May I pre-
sume, dear madam, that this is authentic?"

I took some deep breaths to calm myself. Of course
it was "authentic." Handwritten in my perfect penmanship on personal, hand-painted paper created in Mrs.
Wellaver's second-grade class was a very personal confession. One I'd made and written after feeling really
guilty. Perhaps my second-biggest secret ever.

(We must never, EVER discuss my biggest, hugest
secret of all time!)

Becks had kept that note for all these years. She kept it in a scrapbook. Her memory book. Actually, I'd asked her to keep it. See, Becks's mom is always saying how we have to learn from our mistakes. So Becks kept something embarrassing about me.

And I kept something embarrassing about her.

So why did some spy for Weasel have my note?

He said, "M'lady, beware. My spy made this copy. After school today they plan to take the original to the printer's shop down on Orchard and McIntosh." Weasel told me that they were going to make **REALLY GINOR-MOUS POSTERS** of my confession and use them to destroy me and democracy!!!

Pure *eee-vill!*

How could Rebecca do this to me?

"Fear not, dear lady. If you will allow me to assist, I have a plan. But you mustn't let on. Not yet. Meet me near the bike racks. I know just what to do!"

"Weasel, what do you want? I know you want something or you wouldn't be trying to help me."

Now my hands were on my hips. When Weasel smiled it made you rethink everything you ever thought about how nice a smile could be. His lips were thin and cracked and his dark hair was slicked away from his pale face. It was like making nice with a ghost.

"Oh, dear girl, it is not what I want from you but truly what you can have if you let me help you."

"Like what?" I crossed my arms over my chest.

"Money and power! Not only can I help you win the election, but I can help you become the professional cupcake baker you've always dreamed of being."

My mouth went dry.

Weasel rubbed his greasy palms together.

"Trust me," he said. "I know just what to do!"

16

A Political Race!

It was like something out of a spy movie.

With me, Lauren, and Sara as the good-girl secret agents. And Jasmine Moon and that turncoat Becks as the evil villains!

At the bike racks a bunch of kids were hooting and hollering, being noisy and loud like usual. I told Sara and Lauren about the note. I also told them I thought Rebecca Rat Fink Harper had sold me out.

Sara's arms were folded tight across her body, and her face did not look happy. "Okay, look, we get it. Rebecca did something that's not cool."

Lauren bit down on her lower lip and glanced at Sara, then said to me: "If she did this, it was *so* not cool."

"But," said Sara, "we're not going to be friends with Weasel to help you get back at Becks. No way."

"She's one of our best friends. Yours, too," Lauren said.

"She sold me out to that crinkly-haired vote-stealing Jasmine Moon. How could she do that?"

"Maybe there's an explanation," Sara said.

Right then, Weasel showed up.

"Um, my dear ladies, it is imperative that we..."

"Shut up, Weasel!" Sara and Lauren said together.

"You guys, he's helping me. Helping us. You want me to win, right?"

Lauren's eyes got even rounder. "Look, B., we're with you a hundred and ten percent. But Weasel is...such a *weasel!*"

"He told that lie about us last year and everybody laughed at us for a long time. C'mon, Bree. Just because he's never lied about you, doesn't mean you should trust him!"

Weasel slicked back his greasy hair. He said, "Sorry, ladies. An honest mistake."

He didn't look sorry.

Sara said, "He went around telling people we tried

to get married to our teddy bears and we used to practice kissing them. KISSING THEM! I was *sooooooo* embarrassed!"

"Sara...," I started, but right then, Weasel tugged on my sleeve.

"That's him!" He pointed to a chubby kid on a too-small bike wearing a helmet with orange and yellow flames on top. Jasmine walked up to the boy and handed him a large, yellowish envelope—the kind that teachers use sometimes in class. As soon as Weasel pointed at them, they all looked our way—Chubby Bike Boy, Jasmine Moon, Tabitha Handy, and REBECCA.

Weasel jammed on his helmet and took off on his bike, and I was right behind him. As soon as they saw us coming, Jasmine Moon shouted to Bike Boy, "Go! Go! Go!" Our eyes met and hers sparkled with pure *eee-vill!*

"He's getting away!" shouted Weasel.

And the boy started pedaling hard down the block.

Weasel's bony arms and legs reddened as he pedaled after the boy. When I rolled past where Becks was standing, I yelled, "How could you?"

But I didn't stick around for an answer.

The sun was warm on my arms and legs and face. I

could hear the sound of Weasel wheezing. Lauren's and Sara's bike tires churned through gravel coming from behind me.

At the corner of the fence surrounding the schoolyard, Chubby Bike Boy spun out to make a right turn. Dust and gravel flew into the air.

Weasel pumped harder. His bony knees poked against the fabric of his jeans.

"Catch him!" Lauren yelled, and the next thing I knew she was right beside me and we were racing toward Weasel as Weasel raced toward the boy as the boy raced toward the printer and the end of my political career!

We were approaching an intersection. I said, "We have to slow down! We can't just race across the street without looking."

"Be strong, m'lady!" Weasel yelled. "That miscreant with the harmful evidence most surely will not stop." Why did he have to talk like that? Wasn't it bad enough that he looked like a weasel? Did he have to act like one, too?

Chubby Bike Boy was going really fast now. The sidewalk sloped and slanted so that as soon as you crossed over the big crack in the pavement, it went downhill.

"Watch out!" I yelled.

Through the chain-link fence I could see a blue convertible car rolling along, music blaring. Rolling right toward the intersection.

At the same time, Sara must have spotted it, too. She screamed, "STOP!"

But the kid didn't stop. Neither did Weasel. It took only a few seconds for the boy to shoot into the street. At the same time, the squealing sound of car brakes and the scream of a car's horn filled the air.

At the last second, Chubby Bike Boy jacked back on his brakes. He stopped so hard and fast that the bike shook. Weasel was right behind him and nearly crashed into him.

The man driving the car turned out to be a teenager. Probably from the high school around the corner. "Little Dudes, you okay?" He was out of the car and running over to Weasel and Chubby.

That's when both Weasel and Chubby realized that the big yellowish-brown envelope had flown through the air and sailed to the far side of the street. They both jumped off their bikes, broke away from the teenager, and started scrambling toward the envelope. Weasel grabbed it and tucked it against his chest, but the boy was bigger and stronger and he ripped it out of Weasel's hands.

"Ladies! Some help, please!" Weasel said.

Sara and Lauren both got off their bikes and started moving into the road.

Chubby Bike Boy had the envelope, but Weasel smacked it out of his hands and it once again went sailing. This time right in my direction. Hallelujah! Just as I bent to pick it up...

SWOOP!

Blurred yellow flashed before my eyes. The loud crunching gravel screamed in my ear as the wheels of a skateboard zoomed past. Its rider bent without stopping and snatched the envelope off the pavement. Toady Todd Hampton.

He grabbed it and took off. Now I could hear Jasmine Moon and her Moon Bots clucking behind me like evil chickens. And that made me *soooooo* mad!

Todd looked back at me and grinned. "They told me about your dirty trick. Now it's my turn!" Then he bent his knees and his skateboard shot off down the hill toward McIntosh Lane. And I shot off after him on my bike.

I could hear my name being called in the background, but I couldn't stop. I pedaled hard and fast. Todd might be a toad, but he knew how to handle a skateboard.

"Todd! Give that back!" I yelled. We were a block away from the printer. And we were approaching another intersection. At the corner of McIntosh and Summerville, a group of kids stood waiting to cross at the light. I had to get there before the light changed and the kids started out into the street.

When Todd reached the crosswalk, he snapped the skateboard up and looked back over his shoulder. I'd be right on him in a few seconds.

...Three...two...one...NOW!

I braked, reached out, and caught the back of his jacket. The light changed and people started moving. Big kids who were picking up their little brothers and sisters talked on cell phones or with other big kids. Sunlight turned silver hubcaps and bumpers into shiny bling bright enough to blind you.

Light reflected into my eyes, and Todd snatched his jacket out of my grasp. Then I heard the growl of skateboard wheels digging into the concrete as Todd the Toad used all his leg muscles to make the board go faster and faster. I crossed the street right on his tail, but he was off the board faster than I could get off my bike.

"Todd, wait!" I cried out.

He hit the door and it swung open and he turned to walk inside. But instead he turned completely around and held the big envelope against his chest.

He gave me an evil grin and said, "You'll never be president now!"

Then he went inside and stood in line behind two people. I was about to go in and try to take the envelope. I was desperate.

But by then Sara, Lauren, and Weasel had caught up.

"We have to get inside. We have to stop him!" I said.

Jasmine Moon and posse rolled up next. She whispered:

"You're a blue-haired freak! The word is going to be out on you. Everybody will know you confessed! You'll never win!"

"How did you get that note?" I asked.

"Ladies, we must bid adieu," Weasel said.

"But . . . ," I began.

Weasel was making another weaselly face. "Really, we do!"

Before I could say more, he began to roll away from the little print shop. Sara, Lauren, and I followed. My heart sank. Jasmine Moon had already bribed people with her pizza. Now she'd make that note into a big poster and make everybody think I'd meant to get Todd in trouble, which I didn't.

It was just supposed to be a joke! Audrey had been bragging at school that day with her ten dollars and Todd had told her he'd steal it if she didn't put it away. So when I sneaked it out of her bag, I thought it would be funny. But she found out it was gone while I was out of the classroom. When I came back Mrs. Wellaver was acting like she was on *CSI: Miami.* I thought she was going to take our fingerprints.

A few blocks down, Weasel came to a stop. We slid to a stop beside him. "What's up?" Lauren asked. She looked suspicious.

Weasel wore a big, loopy grin that was *annoying.*

"What?" I said. "We lost. They won. I'll never be president now!"

Weasel grinned his weasel grin and his thin lips vanished from his face. "Don't be so sure, m'lady," he said. Then he reached behind his back and pulled out a large yellowish-brown envelope. Just like the one Chubby Bike Boy had.

He handed it to me.

"What's this?"

He just grinned, and Sara and Lauren twisted around to get a peek. I opened the envelope and pulled out...

The scrapbook page with the evidence.

"Weasel...uh, I mean, Raymond, how'd you do this?"

His grin got even bigger and his thin little teeth appeared behind his thin flat lips and he said, "During my unfortunate scuffle with that scoundrel, I managed to switch his envelope with mine. He never knew it!"

Sara and Lauren exchanged glances. Sara asked, "And you're sure they don't have copies?"

"My source assures me they do not. That was the point of today's little...political race."

"And who is your source?" Lauren asked.

Weasel made a *shhh* sound with his fingers over his lips. "My lips are sealed," he said.

I held the big envelope over my chest and could feel my heart racing as though it were still pedaling up and down the hills.

"Come on," I said. "Let's go to my house for a snack and to discuss strategy. They tried pulling a dirty trick on us; maybe we should pay them back!"

17

Playing Dirty

(Tilden accused Hayes of stealing the nineteenth presidency; I don't know if Hayes did, but I know how Tilden felt.)

With just four weeks left until the elections, I stood in the front hall once again rubbing my fingers along the edges of the plaque with Miss Delicious's name on it.

Fifth Grade President Delissa Marshall. (Otherwise known as Miss Delicious!) Her plaque was among three others for her fifth-grade year.

A week had passed since the big chase scene down McIntosh. Since then, life wasn't the same.

I was so mad at first. Then... I got even madder.

But the worst part was when Sara and Lauren came to me with Jasmine Moon and Becks.

Do you know Jasmine Moon had the nerve to say, "I'm really sorry. The whole thing with the note, it was just supposed to be a joke. I wasn't really going to make copies or use it against you."

Are you buying that?

She smiled her sweet, shiny smile. She batted her big bug eyes. No one else had heard her call me a "blue-haired freak" outside the printer. My face got hot and I said, "What about all that smack you were talking about how I was going to lose?"

They all looked at me. Jasmine Moon started blinking really fast as if she was about to cry. "I'm sorry if you misunderstood," she said, and ran off.

RAN OFF! I am not the bad guy, people!!!

Then the next morning, Sara said, "Maybe you should give them another chance."

"Them? Jasmine Moon wasn't my friend to begin with and she won't be my friend now. Can't you guys see she's playing you?"

"What about Becks? She's your friend. Won't you forgive her?" Sara said. Then she and Lauren tried to get me to talk to Becks, which I totally didn't understand, except both of them really hated Weasel and wanted me to stop letting Weasel work on my campaign.

But if it weren't for Weasel there wouldn't *be* a campaign!

Not to mention the whole "I-can-make-you-a-millionaire" thing.

Raymond Wetzel was the son of Lucille Wetzel, owner of Wetzel's Bakery. He said, "My mom says if you want to come by sometimes and make some of your cupcakes to sell, she'll let you display them in her shop to try out the market, at least through the election. She said you'd have to bake them in her big, professional kitchen, though."

So you know a future millionaire such as myself could not pass up that deal.

At bedtime, I clutched Pig Pig to my pajamas and thought about all the different cupcake and frosting combinations that might possibly set me apart. I'd imagine the scent of fresh butter in a dish; the smell of pureed fruits, chopped nuts, batter with fresh eggs whipped smooth and free of lumps.

At school, the extra history homework and extra-credit assignments were adding up. Presidential candidates had more responsibility because part of the election would include the presidential trivia competition.

I avoided the cafeteria at lunchtime. Instead I met with Weasel in the media center to discuss campaign slogans or buttons or other strategies. I hadn't hung out with him this much since day care. Somehow he didn't seem sneaky when we were working together. Sara and Lauren refused to come. Why couldn't they see how much he was helping me?

But even as I asked myself the question, something squirmed in my belly. Like a tiny voice wriggling up from my intestines, all the way up to my ear canal.

You know why, Bree.

I bit the corner of my lip. Of course I knew Weasel could be sneaky and do dirty tricks. I knew he had lied a lot in the past. I knew all of it, but . . .

I wanted to win. And he was helping. Didn't that count for something?

Sara said, "You know, Bree, maybe you should really think about giving Becks another chance. *Please, please, please, please, please!*"

WOW! She went to the rarely used quintuple-beg please.

"I mean, let's face it, if she really wanted to end your chance to be president, she could have told your OTHER secret."

WARNING! WARNING!

My friends knew that the OTHER secret must be kept among a small, EENSY, TEENSY few. I couldn't even think about what would happen if the rest of the school found out!

"Becks sold me out. So you're saying I should forgive her because she could have been an even bigger sellout?"

And that was that—sort of.

Before I could say anything else, a voice came over the loudspeakers:

"Attention, all fifth graders. Would each of the ten candidates for president of the fifth grade report to Mr. Tan's audiovisual lab at one o'clock. Those of you having lunch may finish your meal and report to the office immediately afterward."

Right as I reached the double red doors of the cafeteria, I looked over at the opposite corner. Jasmine Moon was on her feet, no doubt heading to the same place I was going. My lips felt a little numb, and my throat was dry and hot.

She had no right poking around in my business, messing with my friends' minds just to win *my* election.

And then the fear turned into something hard and sharp. It was anger. I was getting mad!

That was when the question popped into my head:

Jasmine Moon, what secrets are you *trying to keep?*

18
From Cold War...
to the Heat of Battle!

"You are live with Annie Darling!"

Lights. Music. A strange sort of heat.

I stared into the lens of the camera and felt a freaky sort of bubble in the back of my throat.

"So, Brianna, tell me, if elected president of the entire fifth grade, how will you and your administration change Orchard Park Elementary?"

Staring into that camera, the bright lights shining on my face, it was like the whole, entire world was waiting to hear what I had to say.

But before I could say anything...

"...And cut!"

That was Mr. Tan. He said, "Thank you, ladies, for

demonstrating an on-set interview. You may return to your seats."

Mr. Tan was talking about the importance of media in American culture. "What you young people say and how you conduct yourselves on camera can have a huge impact on how other students perceive you."

We all sort of looked at each other and Mr. Tan sighed, knowing he was only seconds from putting someone to sleep.

"We plan to film each of you either here at school or at a location where you can demonstrate your unique talents or skills. I must know by the end of the week what you'd like to do. And all of you must be prepared for an interview with Miss Darling," he said, pointing to Annie.

A shiver passed through me. I could see myself behind a kitchen counter, smiling into the camera just like Miss Delicious. Behind me the oven would be filled with baking cupcakes and the smell would be so good and sweet you could almost taste it through the TV.

This was it!

I was going to be a STAR!

(And thanks to several hair washes, I'd be a star with normal, non-blue hair!)

Then Weasel whispered in my ear, "M'lady, my mother's kitchen awaits!"

It was like he could read my mind.

"My mom says we can film you baking at her shop. Just think of it. Not only will you show your superior skills, you'll also be your own commercial. People will see you and want to try your cupcakes. It's pure genius!"

We were in the hall outside the auditorium. Mr. Tan was finished and was sending us back to class. I jumped up and down and high-fived Weasel saying, "I'll be famous, famous, famous!"

Then, the hair stood up on the back of my neck. The kind of feeling you get when you walk past a cemetery at night.

I knew before I turned around who would be there.

Jasmine Moon!

"Miss Moon," said Weasel.

I said, "What do you want?"

She smiled in a way that didn't look too smiley and shoved her hands onto her hips and moved her face too close to my ear. "You're going to lose this election and your friends!"

My belly twisted. Did I eat sea snakes for lunch? I took a step back, but Jasmine just moved closer.

"You better watch it!" she hissed. "Just because you stopped me before I could photocopy your *con-fes-sion,* don't think you'll stop me again. I bet you have more than one secret."

I gasped.

Weasel stepped in.

"Is everything well, m'ladies?"

Jasmine turned and gave him the unfriendly smile. "I'm just wishing Brianna luck. I think she might need it. You both might."

That was pretty much that. A teacher came by and asked where we were supposed to be. Jasmine went from wicked witch to fairy princess faster than you could say "Abracadabra."

We all went back to class.

But that wasn't the worst part.

The worst part came later, at the bike racks. When I told Sara and Lauren what happened, the only thing they seemed to care about was Weasel.

"Get over the whole Weasel thing. Look, I know he's been a pain in the past, but he's being really...nice. He's working hard on my campaign and I need him," I said. "Besides, right now we have bigger problems. We can't let Jasmine win! And what about my other super secret? She's dying to find dirt on me. What if Becks flips out and tells that, too?"

"We just think Weasel is, like, pulling you down," Lauren said.

I took the key out of my coat pocket and inserted it into the bike lock. It clicked and the lock popped open.

"Pulling me down? What does that mean?"

Sara looped her braids behind her ears as she bent down to unfasten her bike lock. She said, "You know, lowering your standards. You're better than this, Bree."

I stuffed my bike chain inside my book bag. I looked at Sara, her eyes in a disapproving squint.

"Better than what? And what standards?" I could feel myself getting hot under the collar. And that's not just an expression. I was actually feeling pretty heated and wanted to snatch the scarf off my neck to get some cool October air.

"Brianna, you know he's a weasel. It's his name. He answers to it. We just think if you weren't spending so much time with him, this whole thing wouldn't have turned into some sort of vendetta between you and Jasmine," Sara said.

And Lauren finished, "Class president is supposed to be about good leadership and values and being honest and the best person for the job. Besides, you promised not to, you know, get too carried away with the election. You're so caught up in your quest to rule the world you're not thinking straight. All you ever talk about or think about these days is beating Jasmine Moon."

"That's because all Jasmine seems to think about is BEATING ME!"

The swirling wind snatched my voice and snapped it in the wind like a flag. Sara's eyes bulged and Lauren looked away.

I drew a deep breath. I said, "You guys, didn't you hear anything I said? Jasmine admitted she was behind that dirty trick. She was so mean and nasty. I can't lose this election. Think about all the things we've been planning. Being millionaires? My cupcake empire? Any of that ring a bell?"

Both Sara and Lauren had their bikes free from the

rack. We were all moving toward the sidewalk. Sara let out a big sigh and when she looked at me, her eyes were sad.

"You just don't get it, do you?"

And before I could answer, she and Lauren rode away—without me!

19

"We Have Not Yet Begun to Fight!"
(Brianna Justice is in it to win it!)

Outside the autumn air had turned crisp and at night I wore my warm socks in the house to keep my toes from getting frosty. The big oak tree outside my bedroom window was losing its bright green leaves. Each day more and more leaves had begun to change from green to yellow. Some were already turning brown.

Everything was changing.

At school, I felt the changes, too.

Sara and Lauren were giving me the silent treatment.

Almost silent.

They said "Hi," but not like friends. They both turned their backs. I sat slumped in my desk drowning in presidential trivia. I couldn't even look at Becks.

And anytime I even thought about how time was ticking away and the election was getting closer and CLOser and CLOSER...my knees got as rubbery as a bad batch of over-rolled pie dough. It wasn't supposed to be like this. Me running for president of the whole fifth grade, that was supposed to be something for all of us. We had it all planned.

I had a goal. I declared it. I wrote it down. I did everything right. So how had it all gone *soooo* wrong?

The first attempt to really talk came a few days later. An elbow jarred my desk. I jumped.

"Is there a problem, Miss Justice?" Mrs. Nutmeg said. She'd been talking about how some guys named Meriwether Lewis and William Clark went to St. Louis or somewhere looking for...I don't know what. It was in 1804. I wondered if the Arch was there then. Seemed a shame to go to St. Louis and not see the Arch.

"Teachers, may I have your attention, please?"

Saved by the intercom. The loudspeaker crackled:

"There are police in the wooded area behind the school. We are asking that all students avoid that area..."

I looked around and caught a glimpse of Becks. She dropped her eyes and pointed for me to look down.

A note.

I "accidentally" dropped my pencil, bent down, and picked up the pencil—and the note.

The announcement continued. We were being warned to stay away from the wooded area behind the school, the one everyone called the Forbidden Woods. Several kids oooed and ahhhed when Principal Beelie announced that the police said the woods "were unsafe due to recent discoveries."

Dead bodies?

Alien space creatures?

The cast-iron kettle used by the lunch ladies to prepare the barfilicious meat loaf?

Everyone had their suspicions about what had been found and whispers sprang up around the room.

I unfolded the slip of paper from Becks. It read:

Can We Talk After School?

"Miss Justice, can you tell me who was the shortest president?"

Oh, snap! Busted again!

Mrs. Nutmeg was standing right at my desk. How did she get there so fast? And I thought we were learning about Lewis and Clark and their big expedition.

"With the presidential and historical trivia competition at the end of the week, you need to consume as much of this information as possible."

All heads twisted in my direction. Becks looked down and I looked busted.

Shortest president... shortest president...

Abraham Lincoln was the tallest—he was six feet, four inches, but I don't know if that included the tall, skinny hat.

"Miss Justice, we're waiting." Mrs. Nutmeg stared down at me.

I stared back.

Then I did what any red-blooded American schoolkid would do—I faked it!

"Um... Wilbur Howard Taft?"

Several kids giggled. Several more went "Ooo, ooo, ooo." That meant two things:

One—my answer sucked lead.

Two—not only did I give a smelly answer, but I gave a smelly answer to a question that a lot of other kids could answer right. **Not good, people!**

Of course, what made the whole thing even worse was you-know-who.

Jasmine Moon.

She not only raised her hand, but stood. Before Mrs. Nutmeg could even call on her, she said, "Mrs. Nutmeg, we never had a president named 'Wilbur.' I think she means William Howard Taft. But that's wrong. He was the, uh, plumpest president."

My teeth clenched. Mrs. Nutmeg, in her perfectly fitted black suit with the white and black polka-dot scarf sticking out of the front, looked down at me. Then she looked at Jasmine Moon.

"Very good, Jasmine. Can you name the shortest president?"

We'd all been studying from the same four sheets of presidential trivia. FOUR SHEETS! Where is the justice? Each day, Mrs. Nutmeg put about five facts on the board and the next day she'd quiz us on those five and another five random facts from the sheets.

Jasmine Moon cleared her throat and bobbed her head. "The shortest president," she said, "was James Madison. He was five feet, four inches and weighed less than a hundred pounds."

Kenny, from my campaign, said, "Hey, I weigh more than that. Maybe I should be president."

Almost everybody laughed. Anger and a big scoop of shame burned through my chair and lit a fire under me. I shot out of my seat. Mrs. Nutmeg looked at me. I said, "That's not fair!"

Mrs. Nutmeg said, "Sit down, Brianna. There was nothing unfair in what just happened, precious." I flopped back into my seat. Most of the time I loved it when she called me "precious."

She said, "You've got to study harder to be ready for the big competition on Friday."

I sprang back up. "I am. Ask me anything else. Come on…" I drew it out in a little whine. Besides, Jasmine Moon was still standing.

Mrs. Nutmeg had started back toward her desk. She stopped in the aisle and spun around. She looked from me to my new archenemy. She said, "You girls want to have a mini-competition today?"

What I was thinking was, *Oh, yeah. Bring it, girlfriend.*

But I just said, "Yes, ma'am."

"Me, too!" Jasmine said.

She told us to come up front. Whoever had the most correct answers after five minutes would win. She set her timer.

"Who was the first president to travel abroad while he was president?"

"Teddy Roosevelt!" One point for me.

"Four presidents have been assassinated while in office. Abraham Lincoln, James Garfield, and William McKinley are three. Who is the fourth?"

"William Harrison!" *Nnnnnng!* Wrong! No points for Jasmine.

"It's John F. Kennedy. Harrison died of pneumonia one month after doing what? Brianna?"

"William H. Harrison died thirty-one days after making the longest inauguration speech in history."

Bing! Two points for me. **NONE FOR JASMINE.**

"George Washington, Thomas Jefferson, and John Adams all collected and played with these. What are they?"

No answer. No answer. No answer.

"Marbles!" One point for Jasmine Moon; two points for me!

"The youngest president ever elected to office was John F. Kennedy. But he wasn't the youngest to serve. Who was the youngest person ever to serve as president of the United States?"

"Teddy Roosevelt!" Three points for me; one point for Jasmine Moon.

And it went like that until the buzzer rang. At first it was as if the whole room went completely quiet. Wally Sandifer was at the chalkboard keeping score. White dust coated the front of his black, silver, and blue Detroit Lions jersey. With his chubby fingers, he pointed, first at Jasmine, then at me.

"We have five points for Jasmine Moon, and eleven points for Brianna Justice!"

I jumped up and down. I pumped my fists. I said, "Oh, yeah! Now that's what I'm talking about!"

"Brianna, precious, you need a lesson in good sportsmanship. Congratulations. Now take your seat!"

Can you believe it? I won and she was still talking to me like I just said George Washington was the first baseman for the Tigers.

Back at my desk, Becks looked up. She whispered, "Good job, Bree."

Then I looked over and saw Sara and Lauren smiling, too. Did that mean we were all okay again? Could we just squash the madness and get back to being friends so I could kick some Moon butt and be president?

Right as I was feeling so high I could touch the sky, Mrs. Nutmeg brought me back down to Earth.

"Keep in mind, girls, today's competition was just an itsy-bitsy taste of the real thing. Next Friday there will be ten of you. And lots more questions. Study hard, ladies."

I could feel the joy and excitement draining out of me.

Beating Jasmine Moon had felt so good. But on Friday, that could all change. Did I know enough to beat everyone else?

Just then a **thwack** on my heel made me look down.

Another note. And this time from Jasmine Moon.

I didn't even look at it. I just ripped it up!

20

"If You Can't Stand the Heat, Get Out of the Kitchen!"

When the bell rang and everybody got into the hall, it was clear that Lauren and Sara knew about Rebecca's note.

"So will you talk to Becks?" Sara asked.

I shrugged. First I had an errand to do.

Lauren moved in front of me. "C'mon Bree, please think about it. Forget about Weasel."

"I will, but I've got to go." I ditched them before they could say another thing. I needed to tell Mr. Tan about filming my cupcake demonstration at Wetzel's. I didn't want to get into it with Lauren and Sara about my plan to spend time with Weasel's mom at the bakery.

I pushed open the door to Mr. Tan's office. He covered the phone's mouthpiece with his hand and said, "Hello,

Brianna. Could you please wait outside my door? I will be with you in a moment."

Then he closed the door in my face and I did what any kid would do—I plastered my ear to the door to eavesdrop.

"...Man spotted in the woods...behind the school..." I heard him say.

The Forbidden Woods!

Then he said, "...Just a poor, homeless person. It's a shame. He'll have to go, sure. But, well, a person's got to stay somewhere." He said some other stuff, but I couldn't hear, then...

The door flew open, and I straightened up and pasted on my most confused expression. "Brianna? Were you eavesdropping?"

"Huh?"

Mr. Tan's bushy brows bounced up and down. Questioning caterpillars.

"Hey, I'm just here because you told me to let you know what I was doing for the presidential interview."

Every kid knows that when you're busted, always find a way to blame the grown-up. I was there because he told me to be, right?

Before he could say anything else, I told him about the bakery, then raced down the hall, away from his office.

As soon as I got to the bicycle racks, I saw that Lauren and Sara had waited for me. I tried not to let them see me groan. I was in a hurry and didn't feel like arguing today.

As in-your-face as ever, Lauren stepped right into my path and started in on me. She said, "Becks had to go home, but she really wants to talk to you. It wasn't her fault."

Then Sara said, "She didn't even know Jasmine had taken the note from her memory book."

Then Lauren, again, saying: "Jasmine says it was all a misunderstanding."

That should be her new name. Jasmine "Miss Understanding" Moon!

Before I could open my mouth, Pansy and Willow ran over. I gulped. Pansy and Willow were two of the four most popular girls at our school. We called them the Flowers. Pansy. Willow. Violet. Zinnia.

And since the Flowers hardly ever ran, I knew something big must be going down!

"Everybody! The police have taken someone out of the woods. Maybe a deranged killer or something scary."

I remembered what I'd overheard outside Mr. Tan's office. I knew it wasn't a deranged killer or anything like that.

Then a shiny black car pulled to the curb, and the driver and passenger got out. Weasel and a lady. Probably his mom.

"Greetings, fair lady," said Weasel.

Now Sara and Lauren turned back to me. Sara's face looked shocked and maybe even hurt. "Bree, c'mon. Okay I didn't want to spoil it, but Becks...and Jasmine Moon wanted to surprise you."

You know my eyes got like ten feet around.

Sara said, "Listen, we had a long, long talk with Jasmine Moon. We think she's really nice."

I rolled my eyes. "Sara, you think everyone's really nice."

Then Lauren added, "Her mom has rented minivans for Saturday's Pistons game. Her dad's giving us tickets. She was trying to invite you. The note you ripped up in class. Look, I know I was riding the girl harder than anybody. You know you're my girl, Bree. But...I don't know. Maybe we really did jump to conclusions. We all hung at her house yesterday and I think..."

I looked at them, bug-eyed.

"You hung out with her? With her?"

Mrs. Weasel... *um*, I mean, *Mrs. Wetzel* leaned down and said, "You are the little girl my Raymond can't stop talking about! I spoke with your mom today."

"You did?" I was shocked.

"Sure. I told her how my Raymond has taken to you. Shy boy. He doesn't make many friends."

"Oh, Mother," said Weasel. He didn't really look embarrassed. He looked like he was trying to fake looking embarrassed. Just so you know, if my mom ever showed up anywhere and said something like that to my friends, I wouldn't have to fake.

"Now, shush, Raymond. Anyway, dear, I'm heading to my bakery and thought it might be good to bring you down and discuss your cupcake business. And Weasel tells me you're going to be on local and school cable TV and you'll want to film at the kitchen."

"Yes, ma'am."

"Well, come along with us and let's go talk about some things."

I turned back toward the others. Up the sidewalk I could hear Willow and Pansy. They were yelling to a bunch of other kids, "We're going to find out the real deal with the freakazoid in the Forbidden Woods."

I started toward the car, trying to block out the Flowers, the Forbidden Woods, and my friends.

Sara said, "You can't leave, Brianna. That stuff can wait. This is more important."

Weasel was holding open the passenger door for me. "M'lady," he said. And bowed.

I looked from one to the other.

President Harry S. Truman once said, "If you can't stand the heat, get out of the kitchen!" Well, I needed to know if I could stand the heat in Mrs. Wetzel's kitchen.

"Guys, we can talk about this later. I've gotta jet."

21

Lewis and Clark: Expedition into the Forbidden Woods!

Before I got in the car, I used the phone to call my mom and dad—you know, just to make sure. After we arrived, Mrs. Wetzel showed me around and introduced me to a few people who worked for her.

The kitchen was *super delish!* (Rachael Ray, another one of my cooking channel heroes, says "super delish" a lot!)

Mrs. Wetzel made me get out a piece of paper and take out my pencil box. I had to make a plan for how much money I was willing to invest into my business and how much I would charge for my cupcakes.

Thanks to Sara's mom, the banker, we'd all been getting good money advice since kindergarten. So far, Sara had saved the most, mostly because she got paid to help her dad give horse-riding lessons.

Sara............$580
Lauren........$545
Brianna......$540
Becks..........$475

"What if I invest forty dollars to start out?" I said. I really didn't want my balance to get below 500 dollars. Mom and Dad had already made it clear that I had to use my own savings to "launch" my empire. I was going to need every penny!

"Okay. For now, to save yourself time and headache, you might be better off buying premade cake mixes, then adding other ingredients you need to make your special recipes."

I decided to make one of my favorite recipes first. I'd need:

yellow cake mix
eggs
butter

water
a few apples (my secret ingredient)
cream cheese
vanilla extract

I showed Mrs. Wetzel my list. She told me that for now she wouldn't charge me a percentage for "stocking" my merchandise in the bakeshop. She said that her business specialized in homemade breads, muffins, and cookies, so my cupcakes were a natural fit and wouldn't be in competition with any of her baked goods. We talked a little longer, she showed me around, then she took me back to school. I needed to get my bike.

"I'll be okay riding home," I said.

As we pulled to the curb, I could see something was up.

"I hadn't expected so many kids to still be around," she said.

I climbed out of the car and said good-bye. I hadn't expected to see so many kids still hanging around either.

Through the trees, I could see the small playground where the younger kids had recess. Then I saw someone pointing my way.

"Look! She's here. It's Brianna."

I ☆ I ☆ I ☆ I

One minute I was getting ready to head home, minding my own business.

The next thing I knew, I was heading deep inside the darkest, dankest, creepiest place ever:

Welcome to the FORBIDDEN WOODS!

David Love, Gretchen Whitfield, Jimmy Hall, Darrick Palmer, and Jasmine Moon—all candidates for president—were arguing about a bet.

"Justice, you in? The bet is anyone not brave enough to go into the woods doesn't deserve to be president!" David said.

David was a big kid with a thick neck.

There were several other kids, too. And they'd all come up with this plan:

If any of the kids running for president didn't go deep into the woods to the old shed—everybody knew about the shed—word would get around that they were chicken.

And in David's words, "Who wants a big chicken for president?"

When Gretchen pointed out, "Not all the candidates are here," thick-necked David had something to say again.

"If they're not here, they don't matter."

But here's the part that was pure yumminess:

Jasmine Moon was scared out of her crinkly-haired little mind.

"This is dumb. I don't think anybody should be going in there. The police were here earlier."

"That's right," said Darrick. "So they should have taken all the crazy, maniac killers out."

"Yeah, they should have," said Todd. "Maybe they did. Maybe they didn't."

Bright pink dots of fear blossomed onto Gretchen's cheeks. "I don't want to go in there. It's getting dark."

David looked at me. "Are you chicken, too? Maybe none of the girls is tough enough to take a dare."

I looked at the others. Besides Jasmine, the other candidates—Gretchen, Jimmy, and Darrick—all looked afraid, too. They thought there was a chance some terrible danger lay beyond the tall trees. But I knew the truth.

Wouldn't it be the right thing to do to just tell everybody there wasn't anything to be afraid of and be done with it?

Then Jasmine Moon opened her big, fat mouth. "Brianna, I know you're scared, right? Why don't we ride our bikes home? I'll tell you what the girls and I are wearing to the Pistons game this weekend."

The girls and I. Really? Steal my friends and then act like we're just one big band of friends?

"Just because you shoot hoops like a dude, that don't make you tough, Bro-Anna." Todd laughed his merry little toad laugh.

That did it.

"I'm not scared. I can handle whatever. And I can handle it better than any 'dude.'"

Jasmine Moon rolled her dark eyes.

Josh, one of Todd's toadies, looked bug-eyed with fear. "I heard the cops took one man away and went looking for weapons. Maybe there are more bad guys in there." Then he started making *wooo-oooo-ooo* sounds like a ghost.

We edged closer, looking over our shoulders to make sure no teachers had come out of the school. Acorns crunched with each step.

"All right, here's the deal. Everybody stay together. You all have to go as far as the shed. Anybody turn around and come out before the others, you're disqualified." Josh was standing on a tree stump. Yellow and red leaves shifted into piles as slow, lazy breezes pushed between the skinny tree trunks. Then the breezes blew harder. A tiny tornado of red and yellow leaves created an orange blur.

A cloud skidded into the sun's path. The woods were growing darker.

Josh swallowed hard. With a shaky voice, he said, "On your mark...get ready...get set...*GO!*"

We took off—me, David, Jasmine, and Darrick. Gretchen and Jimmy were the first to chicken out.

"It stinks back here," said Jasmine. She sniffed. She was a slow runner. We were racing deeper into the darkening woods.

"That's the smell of nature," said Darrick.

"That's the smell of a crazy killer living in the woods," said David. I glanced at him. He glanced at me. His eyes twinkled like he knew a secret.

Right then, the sound of a branch snapping made us

all stop and gasp. We looked toward the sound, but with so many trees and shadows, we couldn't see a thing.

"It's nothing. Let's go!" David started running again and I ran to catch up. Jasmine hesitated.

"How do you know it's nothing?" she said. She looked so scared. I felt guilty. Maybe I should just tell her what I'd overheard outside Mr. Tan's office.

Darrick started to run, but not fast. He said, "It's probably nothing," sounding as though he wanted to convince himself.

We were running harder now. David was fast. But I was faster. I loved running. I wasn't thinking about crazy killers or homeless people. I was thinking how great it felt to have crisp, cool air rushing into my face. And how exciting it was to race with the others with the tingle of adventure making my skin prickle.

Then:

CAW! CAW! CAW!

Light slanted through the branches above as a gaggle of blackbirds swooped into the gray sky. It was as if I'd fallen into the pages of an adventure story. I was caught up in it.

So I said, "Maybe that was the killer?" Then I screamed. It wasn't a scream-scream. You know, not an I'm-scared-out-of-my-mind scream. It was an I'm-so-psyched-I-could-scream scream.

Not for Jasmine. She shrieked. A real I-think-I'm-going-to-die shriek. Darrick made an awful sound that was part gasp, part gurgle.

Jasmine's face looked ghostly pale behind a freckled curtain of leaf shadows. She said, "This is so dumb. I'm getting out of here!"

Darrick paused, looking at her. David and I looked at each other and shrugged. "I'm going to the shed," I said.

David looked at the others and said, "Later."

The shed was really close. We kept running. My heart was pounding faster now. I'd scared myself. What if the homeless guy hadn't been the only one in the woods? What if someone else was really out here?

I ran harder. David breathed hard beside me.

"There it is!" he said.

We both ran as hard as we could. Then we slapped the side of the shed with our hands.

"We did it!" he said. And we gave each other high fives.

Running out of the woods, we went a little slower than we had coming in. Then David said, "I'll race you!"

We broke into an all-out sprint. We were running and giggling and talking trash. Stuff like, "You can't hang with me...I'm going to smoke you...I could beat you with one leg tied behind my back."

By the time we got to the edge of the Forbidden Woods, we were laughing with our mouths open, running as hard as we could.

Running so hard that we ran right into Principal Beelie.

All the other kids were gone. It was just me and David. And the principal.

22

President John Quincy Adams
Caught Swimming Naked
(Still, it's not as embarrassing as getting caught racing through Forbidden Woods.)

Good morning, students of Orchard Park Elementary. Today, stunning developments in the race for president of the fifth grade.

Your reporter, Annie Darling, has learned that several candidates representing several classes were caught racing in the area to the south of the school, otherwise known as the Forbidden Woods. Now, although Dr. Beelie has asked that the names not be released on TV-One, we all know that at two p.m. yesterday there was an announcement made on this very channel asking all students to avoid that area because our principal had made it off-limits.

How these events will affect the election . . . we will just have to wait and see. I'm Annie Darling and that's the morning announcements!

I ☆ I ☆ I ☆ I

I slumped even further down in my seat. We'd learned earlier how President John Quincy Adams used to swim naked in the Potomac back in the 1800s when he was president. And a lady reporter came to interview him and refused to give him his clothes back till she got her interview.

Gross, right?

Well, I had a feeling how President John Quincy Adams felt. He had to be totally and completely embarrassed when the reporter chick showed up out of nowhere and hid his clothes. I wasn't naked, but getting caught by Principal Beelie had been extra embarrassing.

First, let me just say that now, no one was talking to me. At least, none of my friends. Sara and Lauren gave me big attitude when I got to school today, saying I blew them off for Weasel. It wasn't even like that.

They were the ones who were dead wrong. Not me. Thinking I would ever go to a Pistons game with tickets from **pure e-villllll**. Who could enjoy the game sitting next to Jasmine Moon?

After Annie Darling's scandalizing news report on the school TV channel, whispers buzzed like angry bees.

At lunch, before I could slip out of the cafeteria and into the media center, I saw Sara and Lauren eating with Becks. A stabbing pain jabbed at my chest. It hurt to see them together—without me.

I had never felt so...alone. I was running for president. Baking cupcakes for sale. Following my plan and working on my goal.

And I had never felt so miserable.

It was clear that the only one waving me over for lunch was Weasel. At first, that thought made me want to droop my shoulders and drag my feet. Instead, I held my head high and marched toward Weasel like I didn't even care.

Anyway, I was trying not to sink into utter despair, *until*...

"So, Brianna. We heard about what happened," said Pansy.

"We think it's cool how you were the only girl brave enough to race into the woods with David Love," said Willow.

After that, the Flowers asked me and Weasel to come sit with them. And the jocks. And the dance team. You know, THE MOST POPULAR KIDS at Orchard Park. Everyone called them the *It Squad*.

And as soon as we sat down, they all started talking about the election, telling me how much they wanted me to win.

Even other candidates like David and Darrick chimed in. They said they didn't even really care about the election one way or the other, they just ran because "everybody expected we would."

I didn't get it. If they didn't really want to be president, why'd they let themselves get nominated? What if one of them really won? What kind of president would they be if they didn't even want to be there?

Pansy twirled the ends of her hair and looked as if she knew what I was thinking. She said, "Hey, somctimes you just do the stuff people expect. Like David and Darrick are the most popular kids in their classes, so of course everybody was going to vote for them. Didn't mean they wanted the job."

Then they all started talking at once, saying everybody

at school figured I'd win. That I was the only person running who "made sense."

"You know when you win, you've totally got to pick the best kids to take with you to D.C.," said Pansy.

And it went on and on. Everybody wanted to pitch in, give me the four-one-one on other people's campaigns. Help with signs. Help with fashion advice for my big TV appearance. Tell me how to spend the fifth-grade class money that could be used for any school activity.

"I think it would be totally cool to have a winter beach party!" Zinnia said. She went on and on about it. How she'd seen it in some movie and we could have inflatable pools and sand brought in from the hardware store. And play beach music and do all this crazy cool stuff. By the time she finished, I felt like I'd be crazy *NOT* to have a winter beach party in the cafeteria.

Willow gave a deep, dramatic sigh and tossed her napkin onto her tray. "Maybe you could, like, get them to have decent lunches. This stuff is gross. I'm diabetic and there's almost zero here I can eat."

Pansy rolled her eyes. "That's right, Willow, it's always about you. No one's going to spend the fifth grade's money that could go toward a rockin' beach party on something dumb like lunch."

After that, there was a lot of laughing and falling all over each other like we were the best of friends. All the while I could tell the whole thing was really tripping out Sara and the others. One part of me felt like, that's what you get. You're totally ditching me when I didn't do anything wrong. That part made me laugh hard and loud and act like I was having the biggest, best time of my life.

But here's the weird part:

Instead of that making me feel good, all I felt was even lonelier. The Flowers, the dance team, all of the popular group were kids I knew. But I'd never really cared about them. I had never really cared what any of them thought. Now, here I was, sitting with them while they went on and on. I felt as if I'd taste-tested too much frosting and might have to puke.

I couldn't stop thinking about how my whole life was totally flipped out and freaky. I mean, me, Brianna Justice, part of the It Squad?

Pansy pulled out a mirror and looked at herself, then held it to my face and said, "Your dimples are really super-cute. Be sure to show them a lot when you're on television!"

I looked at myself. It was my face. A kid version of my mom's face. But wanna know something freaky?

It was like the girl looking back at me was somebody I didn't even know.

23

Baby Ruth: More Than a Candy Bar!

Butter.

The sweet, soft scent of butter was all around me. I inhaled and let my mind float away on a buttery cloud sprinkled with finely granulated sugar. Rectangles of cream cheese blocks softened to room temperature, their silver foil packaging glinting off bright overhead lights.

I yawned. Through the skylight I saw navy blue sky and few stars. It was so early in the morning, I could barely see at all. Who knew that to make it as a world-famous cupcake chef you had to get up at 5:00 a.m. The only thing I was used to seeing at this time of morning was my dream of becoming a chef.

Last night, after dinner, Mom and Dad came to my room. They told me they were happy that I'd be getting a chance to be a real chef at Mrs. Wetzel's bakery. Then they laid down the law. "If your grades slip one bit, young lady, we're pulling the plug."

They'd both given me the stern face and told me I'd still be expected to keep up with my schoolwork, homework, and chores.

I should have been having the time of my life. I was baking cupcakes in a professional kitchen, preparing to sell them. It was my dream come true!

Instead of jumping for joy, all I could think about was tomorrow's big trivia competition.

I HAD TO WIN!

And I was thinking about something else, too. The cafeteria. Lunch with the It Squad. I kept thinking how most of the kids who were running were only interested in doing it because they were popular, not because they thought they'd make a good president.

That wasn't like me at all, was it?

Blades whirred. Chunks of sweet Red Delicious apples and tart green Granny Smith apples churned and ground and blended in the food processor. Were Sara and

Lauren right? Had I let the idea of beating Jasmine Moon become more important than anything?

Was that the only reason I wanted to be president? I pushed the Stop button and silenced the grinding blades. Then I felt a hand on my shoulder.

"Aaaaargh!" I shrieked, spinning around.

"My goodness, child. Why so jumpy?" It was Mrs. Wetzel. I took a deep breath, then blew out a sigh.

"Sorry," I said.

She looked at me, then gave me a gentle pat on the shoulder. "Don't be nervous about displaying your product in the bakery. You'll be fine. We'll start out with two dozen and see how we do. I'll pick you up after school today when I fetch my Raymond. Won't that be exciting?"

I gulped. The pit of my stomach boiled like I'd just swallowed a mouthful of Scope. I said, "I can't wait." Then she picked up an armload of large silver bowls and headed across the busy kitchen.

When I reached across the island to open a package of cream cheese, I couldn't help thinking about my girls—Becks, Lauren, and Sara. It would be so cool to have them in here. Becks would be all careful and a little shy, like always. Sara would measure each little ingredient as if we were in science lab doing some sort of experiment. And Lauren would have to get her finger slapped several times for tasting too much batter. And all the while, we'd be laughing our butts off.

Instead of that, though, I was jittery from too much coffee and woozy from not sleeping and having too many nightmares.

I shook my head and plopped the sweet-scented cream cheese into the food processor along with a stick of butter. I needed to prepare for the quiz, not worry about my friends. Between serving my in-school suspension, not to mention the many hours it took to concentrate on how mad I was at my so-called friends, I had hardly any time to study my presidential trivia sheets.

And when I did study, I always seemed to drift off to sleep. Still, I was so nervous it was making it hard to get a decent night's sleep. Last night at dinner, I actually used the word "fortnight." When a kid starts talking like that, you know she's spending too much time in the history workbook.

I'd heard kids talking about how cool Jasmine Moon was for taking a group of "friends" — kids who were supposed to be my friends — to the Pistons game.

I jammed my fingers into the Mash and Crush and Whip buttons on the food processor, again and again, until I couldn't even hear myself think.

For the next two hours I let my cupcakes cool, finished two batches of frosting, then topped the yellow cakes with rich, creamy frosting. Since I hadn't been able to go to other bakeries and check out their cupcake displays, I'd used a book Grandma gave me last year. It was full of cupcake recipes and pictures.

My recipe was inspired by our great nation. Everybody knows that the great American dessert is apple pie.

So I'd come up with an apple pie cupcake.

I separated the frosting into three bowls. In one bowl, I added red food coloring. In another, I added blue food coloring. I glanced at one of the facts on my study sheet:

Many people believe the Baby Ruth candy bar was named after famous baseball player Babe Ruth. Not so. It was named after President Grover Cleveland's oldest daughter, Ruth Cleveland.

Just like Teddy Roosevelt and the teddy bear, President Cleveland's daughter had had something named after her, too. Maybe I should add candy bar chunks to my next recipe.

After I finished stirring the food coloring into the two bowls, I had red, white, and blue frosting. I added one stripe of colored cream cheese frosting to each cupcake, then another and another.

This time, when I looked up, morning light had begun to sift down from the skylight. I'd finished two dozen cupcakes, including sparkling red and blue sprinkles.

"They look great!"

I jumped.

"Hey! You've got to calm yourself," said Mrs. Wetzel. She gave me a quick hug and then pulled back and looked at my face. I tried not to let her see how worried I still was.

She said, "You have a fantastic business plan. You've made your investment. We will sell your first twenty cupcakes for a dollar-fifty a piece. If they all sell today, you'll earn back all the money you spent on supplies." We were selling only twenty because she made me take out four to test and share with the staff. Everybody said they were really good.

Mrs. Wetzel loved business. I could tell. Whenever she talked about this stuff, her round, pink cheeks got pinker and her greenish eyes sparkled like glitter. One good thing had happened: getting to know her was letting me get a real inside look at how a cooking business worked.

I had to admit, it was harder than I'd thought. You never got to sit down and you had to get up really early to make sure you had fresh food to place in your case that day. The smell of baking bread, bagels, and muffins filled the room. I started cleaning my area. Mrs. Wetzel said, "Once you're finished, I'll take you to school."

I nodded. Now, instead of thinking about presidents, my mind was on my money.

Supplies
2 boxes cake mix = $2
18 eggs = $1.89
4 sticks butter = $3
1 box powdered sugar = $1.50
2 apples = $1.20
1 box graham crackers = $2.28
1 package cupcake cups = $1
(food coloring and sprinkles from home)
TOTAL = $12.87
If I sell all 20 cupcakes for $1.50, I'll make $30.
$30 - $12.87 = $17.13

That means I would more than double the money I spent. And since I had another box of mix and all the rest of my ingredients left except the apples, I could wind up doubling my double, which would be excellent.

Mrs. Wetzel said how well they sell will determine how often I will come in and make cupcakes.

If I want to start an empire, I'm gonna have to make a lot of cupcakes.

I sighed, spun around, then went, "Aaaaaahh!"

"M'lady, Mother says you're extra jumpy today. I come with good tidings."

Weasel! Funny thing. For some reason, I thought spending more time around his mom and seeing him out of school would explain the weirdness. But no. No, it did not.

"I didn't even know you were here," I said. My heart was doing hopscotch.

"How are you doing with your trivia competition studies?" he asked.

"Um, uh..." What could I say to sound more confident than I felt? Weasel was staring like I'd just jumped out of one of the bread loaves. I decided to just be honest. "No. I mean, I have been studying, but I'm getting worried. What if I haven't studied enough to beat her? Well, not her. I mean... you know, everybody."

He stepped closer. "*Shhh!* Do not even say such things, m'lady. Losing is not an option."

I rolled my eyes, saying, "I've had a lot on my mind."

"Well, fear not. At lunchtime, meet me at the bleachers in the gymnasium. I may have just the right— *answers!*"

That sick feeling was stronger than ever. Somehow I knew I wouldn't like what he had in mind!

✿ Brianna's Cookbook ✿

Apple Pie Cupcakes with Cream Cheese Frosting

1 box yellow cake mix (see instructions on box for ingredients)
1 sweet red apple
1 tart green apple
graham cracker crumbs
1/4 cup melted butter
cupcake pan liners
1 teaspoon cinnamon
1/2 teaspoon nutmeg

Frosting:

1 8-oz. package cream cheese
1 stick salted butter
1 cup confectioners' sugar
1 cup milk
1 teaspoon vanilla flavoring

If you like apple pie, you'll love this. And it's really easy!!!

First, with your parents' permission, use a food processor to mince the apples. First, peel each apple, then mince each separately and set aside.

Second, combine the required ingredients and follow instructions for your box of cake mix. Take a half cup of sweet apple (minced) and a half cup of tart apple (minced) and gently fold into your cake batter. Now set batter aside.

Next, spread 2 cups of graham cracker crumbs onto waxed paper. Add cinnamon and nutmeg. Use fingers to mix. Add melted butter and squish it together until all crumbs are moist. Fill each cupcake liner with a teaspoon of crumb mixture. Fill remainder of liner with cake mix. Once you've filled your cupcake pan, take any remaining crumbs and sprinkle them on top. Then sprinkle the leftover minced apples on top.

Bake according to cake mix instructions. Remove; test with toothpick. They will probably need an additional 10 minutes to ensure individual cupcakes are done through.

When done, remove from oven. Wait 5 to 10 minutes, then remove from pan onto cooling rack.

To prepare frosting:

Cream the butter and cream cheese together in a bowl (that means use a mixer and mash them up together until you can't tell one from the other).

Add the vanilla flavoring. Carefully add the confectioners' sugar and milk. The cool thing about confectioners' sugar and milk is that there's really no wrong amount. If you want the frosting wetter or more loose, you add more milk; if you want it stiffer, you add more sugar. It's my favorite.

When cupcakes are cooled, spread some frosting on and your mouth'll whistle "Yankee Doodle Dandy"!!!

24
Tricks and Traps!

Everything was getting on my nerves. I just wanted to get this day over.

Mrs. Nutmeg left for a teacher's meeting the first few hours of class this morning. The teacher next door, Mr. Ketterman, would pop in on us every so often. We were supposed to be studying and going about our normal morning routines. I was studying my math and trying to ignore Toady Todd. He kept walking up and down the rows sniffing and saying, "I know I'm not the only one who smells it. Cake. Somebody in here's got cake. I want some cake!" I smelled like a bakery, I knew it, but was too tired to say anything.

Anyway, I was ignoring him—him and Sara and

Lauren and Becks and the entire Moon Bot squad, including the Main Moon herself.

Of course when Mrs. Nutmeg came back and the desks were all every which way and people were out of their seats, she went bananas. When she got through yelling, she said, "Brianna, you're up first today."

I went to the front.

"We'll use the projector, Brianna, like I told you. Pull down the screen, please," Mrs. Nutmeg said.

I was supposed to talk about presidents and their pets as part of the presidential trivia competition. My eye twitched. It wasn't that I didn't know what to say, because I did. I'd given my information to Mrs. Nutmeg yesterday and she'd written it on one of those sheets made for the overhead projector.

Anyway, I wasn't nervous, just jittery. It didn't feel right being up there and not wanting to make eye contact with my own friends. In fact, being up there just reminded me how jacked up my life was and I just wanted to squash the *foolishness* and make everything go back to the way it was. I was all ready to talk about how William McKinley had a parrot who could whistle "Yankee Doodle" and Herbert Hoover's son had two pet alligators in the White House and John Quincy Adams had one pet alligator and Thomas Jefferson kept caged bears on the White House grounds that some explorer dudes named Lewis and Clark brought from someplace out west.

And I already had so much on my mind. You know, worrying about the stupid trivia competition and whether or not I'd ever get my friends back or whether I'd even want them back and wondering if anybody would want to buy my cupcakes. Which is probably why I wasn't even paying attention when I reached up and pulled down the string connected to the projector screen.

So excuse me very much if I failed to see the slithering beast of doom otherwise known as Taurus the snake wriggle from beneath the screen and plop onto the top of my head!

I screamed so loud that my throat burned.

My hands slapped at it, and I started to run and turned around and around and finally flicked it off me. I leaped toward the door, but I didn't get the door open in time and wound up knocking myself in the head.

I had to go to the nurse's office. As she bandaged the ugly bump, my cheeks burned with embarrassment as I thought of how everyone had laughed at me. It was horrible. As I was leaving the nurse's office, I saw Weasel and told him what had happened. I didn't think I could go back to Mrs. Nutmeg's room. They'd told me I could spend the rest of the day in the media center.

But I needed to study my trivia facts.

At least, I thought I did. *Until...*

Weasel said he'd talked with someone the night before who'd made an anonymous call offering the answers to the trivia competition.

"I'd be cheating, Weasel. That's not how I want to win. And what if I get caught?"

"After what happened in your class today, do you think you can go back up there and concentrate? Do you think you can absorb enough facts about our great presidents to distinguish yourself as a victor in tomorrow's contest? How about we take the answers now, and we can decide later how we will use them—or *if* we will use them." Don't you just love how some people throw the word "we" around when they're getting *your* butt into trouble?

So that was how I wound up with four pages of trivia competition answers the day BEFORE the quiz!

25

"I Am not a Crook!" Says Nixon
(and "I am not a cheat," says Brianna).

My cupcakes were a hit at the bakery, but all I could think about was the answer sheet stuffed inside my book bag.

Was I a cheater?

Would I cheat to win?

That afternoon at the bakery, I could barely keep my eyes off the book bag. Mrs. Wetzel told me the cupcakes sold out at lunchtime. We talked about my future schedule and how she wanted me to proceed. Then she told me she'd spoken with Mr. Tan and approved the school's camera crew to come and "record" me doing my very first "cooking show" right here in her bakery.

I should have been way beyond excited, right?

But the answer sheet...

"M'lady," Weasel said. I rolled my eyes.

"Weasel, please..."

Weasel told me my mom's car was outside and asked if we'd give him a ride. Mrs. Wetzel said she'd be there another hour or more, so I told Weasel "sure."

On the way out, Weasel's thin, hissy voice whispered, "My advice is to just study the answers. For the competition, the questions will be multiple choice—a, b, or c. There are forty answers. Memorize them and you'll be fine. That way, if you get stuck on something, you have the answer sheet to fall back on."

"Weasel, doesn't it bother you at all that this is cheating?"

Not surprisingly, he said he did not see it that way. I climbed in the backseat, afraid that Mom might have some super-secret FBI agent decoder device that would let her detect the presence of a stolen quiz answer key. Hey, she said her kind of investigating dealt mostly with paper crimes.

Well, this was a HUGE paper crime.

"Honey, you seem unusually quiet," Mom said after we'd dropped Weasel at home. "Tell me all about your first big day at the bakery!"

Darkness in the sky had overtaken daylight. Icy aprons of snow scalloped with an overlay of icicle lace stretched up and down the block. Snow had already begun to fall and we hadn't even had Halloween yet.

Halloween was two weeks away, which meant one important thing:

The election was TWO WEEKS AWAY, TOO!

Managing to dodge Mom's questions in the car, all I wanted to do was get out, go inside, and figure everything out.

I knew what I wanted to do.

I wasn't going to do anything.

Using that answer sheet would be wrong. Cheating. I was no cheater.

Mom pulled a few days' worth of mail out of the box and I turned and saw a group of girls up the street, turning our way.

When they were right beneath the yellow glow of the streetlamp, I saw them clearly.

Jasmine Moon!

And with her were Sara, Lauren, a few girls from other fifth-grade classes at our school, my former stalker, Tabitha Handy — and Becks!

179

Jasmine Moon saw me on the porch, my face frozen. She pointed and yelled, "Snake! Snake! Snake!"

Then she burst into laughter, and the laughter stung way worse than the icy air.

Oh, so it's like that, huh? I mean, are you serious? Getting cracked on and laughed at even by my so-called friends. I didn't wait to see how hard Lauren, Sara, and Becks were laughing.

I'd rather be a big fat dirty cheater than a loser.

No way could I let myself lose to Jasmine Moon.

She was going down!

26

George Washington Cannot Tell a Lie
(Can I?)

By the next day, I had pretty much convinced myself that the whole snake in the overhead projection screen thing wasn't an accident. And since Sara and Lauren helped Mrs. Nutmeg every morning with the animals, I thought I knew who had set me up.

What a dirty rotten trick.

If it really was a dirty rotten trick.

I was sure it was the dirtiest, rottenest trick.

Almost.

Before school I yawned and tried to focus as I decorated my second batch of red, white, and blue–frosted cupcakes.

The day before, I'd made a special trip to the market

for fresh bananas, fresh ground espresso, and a few other ingredients. I'd been planning a surprise for Becks, who loved all things banana. Thought maybe we could have a truce and a fabulous dessert.

But no more!

When Mrs. Wetzel asked what I was going to do with my new creation, I shrugged. So she told me I should go ahead and sell them.

Then she wished me good luck in the trivia contest and I tried to keep my answer-key rhyme straight:

"Abba, caba, cccc, ab-ab, abcc; ba-ca, (1, 2, 3), ca, ca, bbb... that's almost the end; don't forget the aabbcc!"

I'd memorized the answer sheet. I'd thought of it like a song.

Now I was sitting in Mrs. Nutmeg's class with a terrible headache and yawning to stay awake because I'd stayed up so late studying.

I caught Jasmine Moon looking at me. She started to whisper "snake" and laugh, but this time, instead of trying to run away like yesterday, I just stared right back. She closed that flopping yap of hers real quick.

It was 10:15 when the office called for all "presidential candidates" to report to the cafeteria. I snatched up my book bag and practically raced out the door.

"Slow down, Miss Justice," Mrs. Nutmeg said. But I didn't. I wanted to get out of there as fast as I could.

Dr. Beelie stood inside the cafeteria wearing that same ridiculous getup he'd worn when he was riding the horse. Including the dopey wig. He looked like a history hairball spit right out of my social studies book.

I felt crankier and meaner than the snake that fell on me the day before. But one thing was for sure, I was going to win today. Thanks to Weasel's secret agent, I had all the answers. Feeling guilty, no doubt, was turning me into a snarling Miss Cranky Thing. I hated Jasmine Moon for making me feel like I had to do this—to cheat. I wasn't a cheater. I was a good person. But the knots twisting in my stomach made me wonder: if I was such a good person, why did I have a greasy cheat sheet memorized and hives breaking out on my neck?

"The trivia quiz is multiple choice, ladies and gentlemen. Please, students, if you know the answers, do not yell them out or answer. Only the ten candidates can answer, and they must ring the buzzer to do so," Beelie said.

Buzzing.

That's what was going on in the back of my skull.

Bzzzzzzzzzzzzzzz. Are you sure you want to cheat?

It was about the answer sheet. Using those answers to cheat was not right.

Bzzzzzzzzzzzzzzz. What if you get caught?

I shut my eyes. Shook my head. I wanted the buzzing to stop. Of course, I didn't want to cheat. But if I didn't, I might lose. And losing stinks, right?

"Before the competition begins," Beelie was saying, "I have a really big surprise for everyone..."

I zoned out again. Kids had started filling the room. Looking around, I spotted Weasel. He was looking as weaselly as ever. Pansy tossed her hair in my direction and Willow mouthed, "Don't blow it!"

"...That is why," Beelie went on, "I am introducing one of Orchard Park's most esteemed graduates, Miss Delissa Marshall, also known as Miss Delicious!"

My heart stopped.

My mouth went dry.

Did he really say...

And there she was. Miss Delicious, in the flesh.

"Good morning, students," she said.

Bzzzzzzzzzzzzz. Would my hero witness the greatest day of my life... or would she see me fall harder than an overcooked soufflé?

27

"The Only Thing We Have to Fear Is Fear Itself."
(Unless you flop in front of your all-time biggest hero!)

Miss Delicious looked like a chocolate angel wearing a creamy white sweater and matching skirt and boots. She stood at the podium with the light reflecting off her soft brown hair.

We were onstage in metal folding chairs, and she turned to us and smiled.

But after Miss Delicious's greeting, I wished I could melt away.

"Students of Orchard Park Elementary, it seems as if it was only a few years ago that I walked these very halls wondering if I'd ever make my dreams come true. Back when I was your age, the only thing more important to me than baking was my friends..."

My face got warm. That was just how I felt, too.

At least, it used to be.

"Being class president wasn't about being the prettiest or most popular; it was about reaching out and helping others. It was about setting a good example. No matter what happens today or on election day, remember that as long as you have conducted yourselves with dignity and honor, you are indeed a winner!"

A few chairs down from me, I caught a glimpse of Jasmine Moon. She stood, along with all the rest of us, held her head high, and applauded like nothing had happened. Hadn't she heard what Miss Delicious said? Now my stomach dropped harder than a pan of lead biscuits.

Over my shoulder I saw David Love and Jimmy what's-his-name high-fiving. Like nothing was wrong.

We were not conducting ourselves with dignity and honor or anything of the sort.

We were behaving like power-hungry . . . *politicians.* We were running AMOK!

But no one seemed to be feeling sick about it except ME!

Before I knew what was happening, it was time to start the competition, and the first question was on the overhead projector, and someone's buzzer was going off.

He was the first president to reside in the White House, moving in in November of 1800 while the paint was still wet. He was:

A: George Washington

B: John Adams

C: John Quincy Adams

My lips felt numb. My hands shook. According to the dirty-rotten filthy cheater's cheat sheet, the answer was supposed to be "a." But I knew that answer. It was "b," John Adams. When George Washington was president, the capital was in Philadelphia, not Washington, D.C.

Before I could press the buzzer, though, Gretchen answered and pushed her glasses back up on her nose.

Kids and teachers started clapping, and more and more questions were asked. None of the answers matched the dirty-rotten filthy cheater's cheat sheet. All the answers I'd memorized were WRONG!

That's when I peeked at Jasmine Moon again. She was smiling at me. An evil, oily, slimy, dirty-trick-playing smile. I had cheated. And what was worse was I'd spent the entire night memorizing the WRONG answers!

After that, it was like my mind froze. Even when I knew the right answers, my tongue felt heavy and I was unable to talk. Twice I rang my buzzer:

He was the first president to die by assassination. He was killed on Good Friday, April 14, 1865. He was:

A: William Henry Harrison

B: Martin Luther King, Jr.

C: Abraham Lincoln

The answer was "c," Lincoln. Martin Luther King, Jr., was a preacher and he didn't get assassinated until 1967. Harrison died of pneumonia after giving the longest inaugural speech in history in the cold and rain. I knew the answers. I knew. I knew.

But when I opened my mouth—*Eeeeep!* I just stood there, the right answer stuck inside my mouth like a Tootsie Roll. A totally stupid expression glued to my face and my heart doing gymnastics behind my ribs.

The questions continued to sail by me . . . **The first presi-**

dent to own a car (William H. Taft)...The first president to speak over the radio (Warren G. Harding)...The only U.S. president to resign (Richard M. Nixon).

All answers I knew; all questions I failed to answer.

Finally it was over and Dr. Beelie announced, "Well, students, you've done a fantastic job. All of you managed to score points. Well, almost all of you..."

Then I realized I was the only one onstage who hadn't answered a single question. I was the only one who had NO POINTS AT ALL! Some kids in the audience started laughing. Dr. Beelie's face turned red. He looked at me and started sputtering some sort of apology, but by then it was too late because everyone in the WHOLE WIDE WORLD, from SEA TO SHINING SEA, was laughing at me.

"Students, settle down, we needn't..."

I didn't hear the rest. I couldn't listen. The last thing I heard was the sound of the metal folding chair tumbling over as I raced behind the curtain, down the stairs, and off the stage. I had to get far, far away from my most awful day ever.

28

From Boom to Bust...to Busted?

Even the teachers and staff felt sorry for me.

Oh, great!

Back before the Great Depression, when people had money and jobs and life was good, people called it a "boom" or "boom time." But when the Depression happened and people lost their homes and couldn't afford food, it was called a big, fat "bust."

And we all know what it means to be busted.

Hello, my life!

After I'd hidden in the nurse's office for most of the day, someone finally got my dad on the phone and explained what a total non-answer-giving **loser** I was and he came and took me home. He kept asking if I wanted to talk, but I kept silent. He got the hint.

Jasmine Moon won the competition.

Would the *foolishness* ever end?

That night I looked so pitiful, Katy offered to do the dishes for me. I couldn't wait to get into bed. I wouldn't swear to it, but if I didn't know better, I'd believe even Pig Pig was ashamed of me.

Who was I?

When Mrs. Nutmeg had asked that question a while back, I felt as though the answer was obvious. I was... *Me!* And I was proud to be me.

But right now I didn't feel so proud. Or sure of what kind of me I was turning out to be.

I had tried to cheat and wound up messing up a competition I might have won if I'd acted like I had some sense. Maybe I didn't deserve to be president. Maybe Jasmine Moon really *would* make a better president.

That thought pressed into my brain. I tossed and turned. Was Jasmine Moon really the best person to be our president? Okay, sure, I'd sunk pretty low, but hadn't she done the same? Was she feeling as guilty as I was? (She didn't look so guilty today onstage!)

Who are you? What kind of president do you plan to be?

Mrs. Nutmeg's voice seemed to whisper against my ear with each crisp autumn breeze fluttering through my bedroom window. I squished the pillow over my ears and kicked the covers off. When I took the pillow off my face, Pig Pig was staring right at me. And that got me thinking, too.

Tomorrow was Saturday. Woodhull Society Saturdays. Only I would be working at the bakery. Not that it mattered. Sara and Lauren had barely said two words to me all week. And don't even get me started on Becks. If they created an Olympics for people trying to avoid looking at each other, I don't know who'd take the gold—me or her. But we'd both be in the running.

I opened the drawer in my nightstand. The envelope holding my last two allowances lay inside. Even having all that cash so close didn't make me happy. I closed the drawer quietly and tossed and turned some more.

All I'd been thinking about for almost a whole year was being president of the fifth grade. I had planned my campaign. Made posters. Practiced speeches. Told everybody.

Being president was going to help me start my future career—cupcake-making millionaire.

But I'd been so excited about what being president would mean to me, I never thought much about what it would mean to the school if I could be president.

I fell asleep trying to figure out if it was too late to turn into the kind of presidential candidate that would make me proud to be me again.

29

Abraham Lincoln, Report to the Battlefield

(Lincoln's important "address" took place on the battlefield; mine begins in the kitchen.)

"I have a surprise for you," said Mrs. W.

I covered my mouth with my hand and tried not to let her see me yawning. I didn't get much sleep last night.

But when I opened my eyes, the grainy "I can hardly stay awake" feeling flew out the back door, past the huge rolling carts, and down the alley.

I couldn't believe it. Standing beneath the skylight, silvery-gray moon dust sprinkling down on her like confectioners' sugar on French toast, was my hero.

Miss Delicious glowed before my very eyes!

I looked around to make sure Mrs. W. saw her, too. A girl couldn't be too sure.

But Mrs. W. did see her.

And do you believe it:

Mrs. Wetzel and Miss Delicious had been friends since their days at Orchard Park Elementary.

"Dee and I, we did everything together," Mrs. Wetzel said.

Miss Delicious!

Right here. In the flesh! How cool was that?

But the grin that was pulling my face fell so fast that both women moved toward me.

"Little Lamb, what's the matter?" said Miss Delicious.

Well, that did it. Stupid, stupid, stupid ol' tears of shame burned at the corners of my eyes and made me blink like a big doof.

I spun around to hide my face, but *Duh!* I was so totally crying.

Miss Delicious wrapped her arms around me and said, "Little Lamb, why the sad, sad eyes? We're all friends here. Between Lucille and me, we've probably made some of every mistake in the book. You're too young to look so tragic! Lucille told me about the contest yesterday. Are you still upset about that?"

I pulled away, shook my head, and began to cry harder.

Now I was a cheater and a crybaby. Was there no hope for me? *I wonder if it's too late for military school.*

"Lucille tells me you're an excellent cook with a bright future," Miss Delicious said, taking my chin in her hand while dabbing a tissue against my wet cheeks with her other hand. "But I'm looking at a young lady who is feeling…something. And it's not success. You'll feel better if you just let it out."

I had to tell someone how awful I'd been feeling. Who better than my hero?

I ☆ I ☆ I ☆ I

So I told them everything. Well, sort of.

I told them how after Miss Delicious spoke to our class last year I figured the only way I could follow in her footsteps would be to become president of the whole fifth grade.

"Now all my old friends treat me like scum and most of the kids who've been hanging out with me only do it so they can get favors if I win. And after yesterday's performance, I bet most of them won't want anything to do with me, either."

Mrs. W. took out two dozen of my cupcakes from the double oven and set them on the counter. "You're being too hard on yourself," she said.

Miss Delicious was stirring my minced apples into the cupcake batter while I spooned the crust for my new election cupcakes into cupcake liners. She said, "Ambition can be a girl's greatest asset, as long as she follows her dreams in a manner that she believes in. My little talk at your school was never intended to give you the impression that the only way to achieve greatness was through fifth-grade presidency."

Mrs. W. gave a hoot of laughter. "For real. If elementary school leadership skills were the secret to lifelong success, goodness knows where I might have wound up," she said.

I smiled. It felt like it had been a long time since I'd been able to smile. "I just wanted to be like you," I said, feeling a little lame, but hey, it was true.

"You flatter me. But one does not make a name for herself in the cooking world or in life by following the path of others. You, my sweet one, must create your own path. You can be a professional pastry chef, a television personality, and a millionaire, but first be a great class president. The question is, do you still want it?"

Do I?

"Miss Delicious, have you ever done something bad? Like really, really bad? And you wished you could take it back, but you can't? Something so bad that maybe you felt like you didn't deserve to wish for anything good ever again?"

She and Mrs. W. exchanged looks, then they doubled over with laughter. "If you're asking if we've made mistakes that either one of us wish we could take back, then, *baaaaybeee,* the answer's absolutely, positively, one hundred percent yes!"

Mrs. W. came around the kitchen work island, still laughing, then straightening and looking more serious. "But if you're asking us how to deal with a mistake, then let's talk it out. We all make mistakes in life, Brianna. How you handle your mistakes is what can determine who you really are."

And that was what I really needed to know. How would I handle my mistakes, and who was I, really?

After we finished up in the kitchen, we drank coffee and talked.

Like any smart kid knows, even when you're feeling all close and connected to grown-ups you don't tell them all the dirty details. Hey, too much information would just confuse them.

But I did talk about my problem at school. My friends had warned me not to get carried away with the election. They had warned me about wanting to win more than I wanted to be a good president.

"Even if you did get carried away," said Miss Delicious, delicately holding the teacup as she sipped her cream-and-sugared coffee. "Even if that's true, you've learned from it. Making that mistake, getting carried away, heck, that just means you're passionate. So what? It doesn't mean you wouldn't make a great president. I think it's wonderful that you're so motivated and that you're a young lady with goals and dreams. But keep in mind, you're a kid. So be a kid. Take your time. Enjoy your life. Play basketball. Hang out with your friends. Don't be in a rush to grow up. Trust me, you'll have plenty of time to make your millions!"

By the time Mr. Tan and his crew arrived with the

cameras, I'd thought a lot about what Mrs. W. and Miss Delicious said.

"I don't want anyone to know before this airs. Not even Weas...um, Raymond. Okay?" I said to Miss Delicious and Mrs. W. They agreed, and I told them my plan.

My new plan.

If I was going to be president of the whole fifth grade, I needed to act like a leader now rather than later.

And with that, I let out a big breath and did my best to start fixing what I'd messed up!

30

This Is for All the Marbles!

"*Psssst!*"

It was Weasel, looking back and forth like he thought he was being followed. What now?

Filming was over and Mr. Tan was gone. So was Miss Delicious. I'd slipped back into the kitchen to grab my book bag, feeling pretty good about my choices. *Until...*

"What are you doing this afternoon?" he asked.

I grabbed my book bag off the bench and slung it over my shoulder. "I've gotta go. Your mom's waiting for me."

"Sorry I missed the filming of your news story this morning. Yesterday, well, it didn't go well. I take full responsibility. But I plan to make it up to you, m'lady."

I shrugged. But Weasel didn't have his normal oily look. His flat brown eyes looked round and... *scared.*

"Are you okay?"

He let out a big sigh. "I really, really let you down. I wouldn't blame you if you didn't let me help you anymore."

Weasel was being so unlike Weasel. He looked sincere. And not the fake sincere face he'd been using since preschool; he looked like he really meant it!

"It wasn't your fault. I'm the one who blew it. I should have just studied and not worried about the stupid answer sheet."

I thought that'd be enough, but he just stood there, looking all skinny and gangly and slouchy.

He said, "I know you think I'm just this weird kid who lives in a fantasy world and who doesn't have a lot of friends."

"But..."

"No, it's okay. Everybody sort of sees me that way. But I've always thought of us as friends. I've always liked how you have friends from all different groups. And you're one of the few people who will be nice to me just because."

I didn't know what to say.

"Weasel...Raymond, don't sweat it. Really. I have a few ideas myself. I don't know if they'll help me win, but I know I'll feel better. More like my old self."

And just like that, the sensitive, sincere Weasel was gone and the oily grin returned.

"Did you know that John Tyler was shooting marbles with his sons when he found out he was president?"

Duh? Like what did that even mean?

"Soooooo?"

"So...maybe you'll be playing basketball or watching TV when you learn what I've done for the campaign."

"What do you mean, Weasel?" An open window let in breezes that cooled the oven-hot kitchen. It also let in the *bonk-bonk* of Mrs. Wetzel's car horn.

"Hey, I gotta go. Your mom promised my mom to have me home by lunch."

Weasel moved closer. "We were right about the lovely Jasmine Moon. She does have a secret. With one week till the election, we still have time to win!"

Then he pushed through the door and ran past his mother's car, crossing the street. I called after him, "Wait! Weasel, I don't want to win like that!"

But he was gone.

A sick feeling burned the pit of my stomach.

A secret.

I'd forgotten all about having that talk with Weasel. It wasn't even a talk, really. Just me being mad, shooting off at the mouth about how Jasmine Moon had used my friend to get dirt on me. Remember how mad I was after Jasmine Moon tried to make me look bad with my secret? Well, I got so angry about her poking in my business that I told Weasel I wondered what kind of secrets Jasmine Moon had. I told him I bet she had some secrets of her own.

Well, I forgot all about it. I never thought he'd go digging around in her past.

What if he did figure out her biggest, darkest secret? Then what? I didn't want to give her an excuse to be digging in my business.

"Can we go any faster?" I asked Mrs. W. I needed to get home.

Something had to be done to stop the *foolishness!*

A true leader needs to make a stand, even if it means losing everything!

31

The Era of Good Feelings
or the New Deal?

All weekend long, I couldn't stop thinking about what I'd done. The news show with Mr. Tan and his crew. And the call I made to try and right a wrong.

"Sara, when we get to school Monday, I need to talk to you, to everybody. Okay?"

Sara sounded surprised but said, "No problem."

It was time to make some changes in the way I'd been doing things. After all, my campaign slogan was *Justice for All.* For the first time since I began my campaign, I was trying to figure out how to make that more than a bunch of catchy words. So I told myself the deed was done. At least, almost done. Might as well not worry about it. When I got home from the bakery on

Saturday, I crashed and took a way-too-long nap. I woke up feeling hungry for a snack and some milk. Katy and I decided to sneak into the kitchen after midnight for ice cream.

Mom and Dad were in there dancing by the light of the opened refrigerator to music that must have been coming from their hearts.

"Uh, gross!" shouted Katy, breaking the magical spell. They looked so happy. I thought they'd yell at us for being up so late, but instead they opened their arms. Katy said "no way" and stormed out. I, on the other hand, could use a hug. I nuzzled into my father's side and felt the warmth of my mother's hand at my back. We stood like that, swaying to a rhythm inside of us for a good long while.

Something about that made me feel, for the first time in weeks, that, yeah, I knew who I was. And I was going to be just fine!

First thing Monday morning I was on a mission. Thank goodness I hadn't heard anything else from Weasel. I was praying that all his snooping didn't actually turn up anything. With one week to go until the big election, I stopped once again in the front hall. My eyes scanned the rows of tiny nut-brown plaques with shiny gold nameplates.

As always, Miss Delicious's name sparkled as though Janitor Bud rubbed it with special cleaners. I slipped my heavy mittens off and traced my finger around the edges of her engraved name. The front halls were decorated with new bulletin boards—several different messages and designs all in red, white, and blue.

This was it, I thought. One week and one day from now the kids at Orchard Park Elementary would cast their votes. My heart started to drum, and suddenly the pounding of footsteps of all the other kids racing through the front doors as they spilled off the buses made my head all get swimmy.

How would everyone react to what I had to say in my recorded biography that would play on school TV later in the week?

"Get to class, Miss Justice. We wouldn't want you being tardy," said Dr. Beelie. He was standing where he stood every morning, directing kids north, south, east, and west.

Since he was a big part of my new Big Idea, I stopped and asked:

"Dr. Beelie, can I talk to you after school today? It's very important."

He seemed to take a step back. He looked me up and down as though expecting I might come to his office and hide fake dog poop in his chair. After a few moments of giving me the suspicious eye, he said to come by his office ten minutes after the final bell.

When I reached my classroom, Mrs. Nutmeg was just about to close the door. I skidded in right after the last bell. Sara and Lauren were over near the aquariums feeding the animals. Becks's seat was empty.

Sara looked my way. I bit my lip. Mrs. Nutmeg glanced at me, looked over at Sara, seemed to think about something, then went back to messing with stuff on her desk. I took a deep breath and marched over to the animal area.

I never go over there.

Sara and Lauren stopped, both staring at me.

"So, can we talk?" I tried to sound casual, but my voice cracked like the top of a cupcake that gets too cold too soon.

"Are you okay, Brianna?" Sara said. "I was ... I mean, we were really glad you called."

Same ol' Sara. Her eyes full of questions. A few strands of hair were loose from the two braids that swung over each ear.

"I'm... I'll be okay," I said. "Um, where's Becks?"

She and Lauren exchanged surprised looks. Sara said, "She's gone for the next few days. Her dad came back from Iraq over the weekend. They're going to visit her dad's family in Chicago."

I smiled and said, "Ooo, he made it in time for her birthday!"

Sara and Lauren smiled too, and in that moment, it was like something very important was happening between us.

"Everybody, please take your seats so we may start our very busy day," Mrs. Nutmeg said.

"I..." The apology got tangled in the back of my throat. Before I could say more, Lauren and Sara closed the lid on the aquarium. Lauren whispered, "Um, we wanted to tell you, that thing with the snake..."

Sara moved closer, avoiding eye contact with Mrs. Nutmeg so she could pretend we all didn't see it was time to take our seats. She whispered, "That was not our fault. We felt really, really bad. I think... I think you were right.

When we went to that Pistons game with Jasmine Moon, all she did was talk about how you thought you were all that and how she was going to have to show you that she was the best."

"Yeah, and we wanted you to know that the other day, Jasmine laughing at you, we weren't part of that. We all feel really bad about what's been happening. We're sorry."

"Girls . . .," Mrs. Nutmeg said.

"We'd better sit. She's wearing her power pantsuit. No telling what she's got up her sleeves today."

We all laughed, but it felt stiff, uncomfortable.

Not like old friends; more like kids trying to figure out what they have in common.

Or if they have anything in common at all.

32
"A Day That Will Live in Infamy!"

For the next few days, being in the bakery was the best part of my day—and kinda the worst.

The best because for the two hours I was in the bakery before school, I was surrounded by things that made me happy. The smell of baking food; the sound of the food processors and mixers whirring and whipping; and taste-testing batter and frosting batches.

The worst part—when I'd leave the bakery, I'd be so excited and happy. I couldn't wait to get to school to tell everybody how cool it was. Only there was no "everybody."

Sure, the girls and I had made up, but we still weren't "us," not like we used to be. Not having them with me like the old times made me feel lonely. Becks still hadn't come back to school. I missed her. I wanted... needed to make things all right between us.

Still, lonely or not, school had to go on, right?

Jasmine Moon's show played on school TV yesterday. She batted her eyes and told Annie Darling how much she loved our school and a bunch of other blah-dee-blah-blah. But when she played the violin, my heart skipped. She could really play.

"Thomas Jefferson, our third president and one of the men responsible for the Declaration of Independence, played the violin, too," she said, just like that day in class, when Becks had played flute.

Then everyone in our class stood to applaud.

All week long candidates had been on the school channel and local cable station making promises, talking about why they'd be the best choice for president. Promises for everything from more equipment for sports teams to more field trips for the fifth grade.

Now it was Thursday. I sat holding my breath as Mr. Tan counted, "...Four, three, two..." Watching myself on the monitor, it was like getting ready for some big game show. In my head I heard:

"Ladies and gentlemen... and toads. Introducing the world premiere television debut of future TV chef and cupcake baker to the stars, Brianna Justice!"

The voice in my head was loud and boomed like the guy in the center ring at the circus. Then the voice went quiet and I held my breath as the prerecorded show of me baking alongside my all-time hero, Miss Delicious, began. Here it was—the moment I'd waited all my life for:

BRIANNA: Hi, my name is Brianna Justice and this is Wetzel's Bakery. I'm here with someone I admire very much, Miss Delicious. Actually, with two someones I admire. Mrs. Wetzel has been very kind to let me come here and make cupcakes to sell.

One day I want to be a famous chef with my own cupcake bakery, and I want to have my own cooking show like Miss Delicious...

Until it was almost over, I hadn't realized I'd been holding my breath. On the screen, Miss Delicious was eating one of my cupcakes and making *mmm...mmm* noises.

MISS DELICIOUS: Brianna, these are fabulous. I love the combination of graham cracker crust and fresh apple filling baked into the tender, moist golden cake, then topped with your amazing cream cheese frosting.... Honey, this is a real winner.

BRIANNA: Thanks. Like I said before, I made 'em 'cause of the election. I wanted to come up with something as American as apple pie. So I created my own apple cupcakes.

I was in Mr. Tan's studio. The Green Room. I was sitting behind a desk that looked a lot like the one newspeople used on real TV. Annie Darling sat next to me. We watched as I talked to Miss Delicious about another cupcake I'd invented, the Itsy-Bitsy Wild Banana Bites. I told her how my friend, Becks, loved anything with bananas and I came up with the recipe because Becks always liked tiny cupcakes.

Anyway, I felt Annie Darling was getting bored. But when the next part came up, I felt her stare burning question marks into my flesh. I kept my eyes on the screen.

Because the scene cut from the bakery to me in Dr. Beelie's office. I'd set it up with Mr. Tan on Monday. After that stunt I'd pulled racing through the Forbidden Woods like a lunatic, sitting down with Dr. Beelie was the last thing I wanted to do. But it was the kind of thing I thought a good leader should do.

So this time I was the interviewer and Dr. Beelie was the interviewee. I told him how all the kids were talking about all the things they could do with the extra money in the fifth-grade budget. But I wanted to know, what did the fifth grade need? What would benefit Orchard Park Elementary School the most?

"Well, young lady, that's quite a responsible and grown-up question. And let me commend you for being the first to ask such a very important question. Now, let's see..." After a bunch of "ums" and "maybes," Dr. Beelie told me that the gym equipment was getting old and cruddy. And he told me he'd like for his fifth-grade president, "no matter who that might be, to come up with a civic project that would benefit the community. I want our young people to understand that being good citizens isn't just about what you can get, it's about what you can give, what you can do for others."

And then, he asked the thing that I most needed him to. He asked:

"So, Brianna Justice, what has participating in this election process taught you?"

Deep breath. Here goes:

"Being in this election has taught me that sometimes you can get carried away with something, you know, spend so much time thinking about winning that you don't spend enough time thinking about how you're going to win or what kind of winner you'll even be if you win."

Dr. Beelie frowned. "Uh, I see."

I tried again. "Dr. Beelie, you don't know this because you're a grown-up and probably don't know as much about what goes on around here as you think, but a bunch of the kids in the election are in it for the wrong reason. They're running because they're popular or because they think that's what everyone around them expects."

"And you, Miss Justice? Do you fall into that category?"

"Sort of. The point is, I've been so caught up in trying to win, trying to make sure certain other people don't win, that I stopped being a good friend to the kids I care about. And I stopped acting like the kind of Me that I'd always been proud to be. That's why I'm here today. I'm hoping it's not too late to try and win the right way and for the right reason..."

Then I told him how a lot of kids were fed up with the cafeteria food and wanted better choices. I told him that I wanted the chance to really listen to the students and hear what they thought would make our school better. I told him:

"Dr. Beelie, I may have made some mistakes in the past, but I want you to know, from now on, I just want to make Orchard Park Elementary the best school ever. As president, I would try to do what was best not only for a small group, but for the whole school."

I ☆ I ☆ I ☆ I

A bright light blazed behind Annie Darling and the desk where we sat. She turned to me.

"Wow! That was amazing, Bree," she said.

Not to brag or anything, but, dang, it was kinda good. I bit the inside corner of my lip. "Thanks, Annie."

"Your video was so different from everyone else's.

You had a famous TV person and former Orchard Park class president. Then *you* interviewed our very own Dr. Beelie."

She slid closer, then asked, "So, what you're saying is you'd rather have your friends than be president?"

I blew out a sigh. "Yes, that's exactly what I mean."

Annie Darling's eyes sparkled as if she'd gotten the news scoop of the century. She said, "So, Brianna, it had been rumored that if you won, you were planning to throw a winter beach party—complete with sand shipped in and inflatable beach balls—to make good on a promise made to your *new* friends. Are you saying now that your plans have changed?"

Good grief! Annie Darling was leaning so far forward I thought for sure she'd fall off her chair.

"Uh, if I win, I won't be having any beach parties." This was it. My chest felt tight and my lips were a little numb. Five days until the voters went to circle the name of the person they wanted as president, and I was about to move away from what Weasel and I had planned and speak from the heart.

"A little while back, a bunch of us got into trouble because we went racing into the Forbidden Woods. Only

I sort of knew they weren't haunted because I overheard Mr. Tan talking on the phone about how the police had arrested a homeless person who'd been camped out back there.

"What I didn't find out until later, though, was that it wasn't just a homeless person. It was a family. A mom, a dad, and three kids. The dad lost his job, the mom got sick, then I guess they couldn't afford a place to live. I found out that stuff when Dr. Beelie got all red-faced, yelling at us for running around in the woods in the first place. After my interview with Dr. Beelie, if I'm elected president, I'd like to talk with the other class officials. Maybe get the school some much-needed gym equipment, then donate the rest to the family from the Forbidden Woods.

"Maybe some students around here wouldn't want a president who would choose to help homeless kids more than having a beach party. But, anyway, that's what I'd like to do."

For about a microsecond I was on top of the world, proud of myself. But I didn't even make it back to Mrs. Nutmeg's classroom before—*DRAMA!*

Itsy-Bitsy Wild Banana Bites

Miniature cupcake pan
Cupcake liners

Ingredients:

1 box yellow cake mix
2 small bananas
2 tablespoons sour cream

Frosting:

1 8-oz. pkg. cream cheese
3 cups confectioners' sugar
5 or 6 tablespoons milk
$\frac{1}{2}$ cup creamed bananas
Dash of vanilla flavoring

Prepare your pan: The easiest way to do it is make sure your pan is clean, then put the cupcake liners—you know, those little paper cup thingies—into the cupcake pan. Trust me, it helps with the cleanup and it's just neater.

Prepare the cake mix based on the instructions on the box. Take the two bananas and sour cream and mash up in the food processor. Add the mixture to the cake batter. Place batter in the cupcake pan, then bake according to directions on cake mix box.

For the frosting, combine the cream cheese, milk, confectioners' sugar, and a dash of vanilla flavoring in a food processor. Then gently fold in creamed bananas.

Allow cupcakes time to cool, then frost.

If you like bananas (like Becks does), then you'll love the Itsy-Bitsy Wild Banana Bites!

33

"President Obama Can Leap Tall Buildings..."

("... in a single bound?")

Did you know that the president, Barack Obama, was a huge fan of *Superman* comics? Grandpa once told me that "...to be the first African American man elected as president of these United States, that young man has to be part superhero himself!"

I tried to picture President Obama in a cape, flying around the country, around the world, making wrongs right. Yeah, I don't think so. President Obama didn't have superpowers, and goodness knows I didn't, either.

Still, me and the forty-fourth president of the United States had something in common—we wanted to fix things that needed fixing. Offering to help people in need, well, that was the start of me trying to fix some stuff that was broken—turning a wrong into a right. Too bad not everybody saw it that way.

"You're not really going to give the money to some homeless family, are you?" Zinnia was almost nose to nose with me.

Pansy rolled her eyes and said, "We were counting on you to win! What about Zinnia's beach party idea?"

They'd stopped me in the hallway on the stairs. I was struggling to hold on to a covered cake pan stacked with my Itsy-Bitsy Wild Banana Bites. I'd brought enough for our class.

Weasel weaseled his way through them and came to stand beside me. "Very touching, m'lady. But as you can see, several of us have an interest in seeing you win."

Pansy gave my shoulder a nudge and I almost dropped the cake pan. "Yeah! He's got an idea to save your sorry behind, so you'd better listen."

"Hey, get away from her!"

Lauren. Sara.

And Becks!

They were at the top of the stairs. Sara yelled, "Back off! She did the right thing!"

Then Pansy and Zinnia turned to look at me one last time, glared, and stalked off.

Weasel slithered even closer. As usual, he was looking left and right as though convinced spies were gonna jump around the corner. He pushed aside a stray, greasy strand of hair. "M'lady, fear not. Despite your lapse in judgment, I have the perfect thing to help you beat your biggest competitor. Miss Jasmine Moon does indeed have a secret worth hiding."

Lauren, Sara, and Becks had pushed past the others and were heading toward me. Weasel leaned closer, his whisper a hot steamy trail on the side of my face. *Ugh!*

"Saturday, at the Halloween carnival, I will reveal Jasmine Moon's deepest, darkest secret. No one will vote for her after that!"

"No, Weasel! That's not what I want."

"Get away from her, Weasel!" Lauren's voice boomed, but Weasel was already bowing and retreating.

"Ladies," he said, before vanishing around the corner and out of sight.

"What was that all about?" they asked.

"That was Weasel still trying to control me and convince me to do anything just to win."

Becks bit the corner of her lip and shifted from one foot to the other. She took a puff on her inhaler. "What are you going to do?" she asked.

"Becks...," I began. The words caught in my throat. I felt rotten about ignoring her for the past few weeks. And I felt rottener about treating her like SHE was the creep instead of me. I took a deep breath and then blew it out.

"I'm so sorry. About how I've been acting, I mean. I should have given you a chance to explain what happened with Jasmine Moon getting her stinking hands on my ... that note."

Becks said, "First, just for the record, I never meant to tell Jasmine Moon your secret about getting Todd in trouble. She found my memory book and saw the letter and the note you'd written under it. She said we should play a trick, but just between us. You, me, the rest of us. She said it would be a funny way for the two of you to get to know each other better."

Lauren snorted. "Oh, yeah, and you fell for that."

"She told me it was supposed to be a joke, Brianna. Honest. I'd never try to embarrass you like that." She took another puff of her inhaler and gave me a sideways grin. "Besides, you have proof of my deepest, darkest secret, too."

"You know I'd never tell. Not ever!"

Lauren said, "And because we're such good friends, we won't even ask what the secret is!"...Five...four...three...Wait for it...two...one..."Okay, I want to know. Please. It's killing me!"

See, that's Lauren. She couldn't help herself. We all burst out laughing. I hadn't realized how much I'd missed that sound. I shook my head. Becks's asthma made her get crazy congestion sometimes. You know, congestion, like when you have a cold and get all yucky with your nose stopped up and that nasty cough? Anyway, in first grade, Becks had one of those stuffy-nosed days while we were on a field trip to the museum. I was taking a picture of her with my camera. She was standing in front of her favorite statue when she started coughing. Right when I took the picture, she sneezed really hard. All over the statue. We were concentrating so hard on using tissues to clean off the statue before anyone could see, that I never checked my digital camera until later. That's when I saw the photo.

Becks was the one who told me to keep it, but NEVER, EVER show it to anyone.

I looked at my friends. My girls. And for the first time in weeks, I felt like my old self. Like a grade-school super-hero.

"Sorry, Lauren. That secret stays with me." Becks shot me a big grin.

"Okay, so what's the plan?" Lauren asked.

"I'm going to put a stop to Weasel and his weaselly ways, once and for all."

Sara did a mini-clap and said, "Yay! Group hug!"

And we group-hugged.

And it felt good!

34

John Quincy Adams Kept
Silkworms as Pets.
(But I bet even he wouldn't put up with a weasel!)

It was not even 5:30 in the morning.

Bad enough I was already in the bakery and still not fully awake. I didn't need Weasel popping out of nowhere with his *foolishness*.

"Weasel, how many times do I have to tell you, I don't want to win if it means acting like this?"

"Ah, yes, m'lady. But as I've told you, there are others who wish to see you win. Others known as the *It* kids. And they are willing to accept me if I can help you snatch victory from the greedy jaws of defeat."

"Weasel..." But he kept going, staring off into nowhere like he was watching some sort of movie with him starring as the evil dweeb.

"Tomorrow, at the Halloween carnival, Mr. Tan has me helping with the spooky DVD that's supposed to play in the background. Well, after a lot of digging, I finally found what we needed. Dirt on Jasmine Moon. Silly little girl used her own mother's cell phone to record her and a friend doing their dirty prank. When the truth came out at her old school—well, let's just say, it's why she had to leave. Once her secret is out, no one will vote for her. None of the other candidates are popular enough to beat you. We'll win!"

He was holding my arm so tight that it started losing feeling.

Once her secret is out, no one will vote for her.

What about my secret? Was there still time for her to find out what it was and blab it?

Or did she already know it? Was she waiting for just the right time to humiliate me one more time?

Pans clanged. We both turned.

"What's going on?" Mrs. W. asked, rounding the corner with cookware.

Weasel immediately threw his arm over my shoulder and pasted on a fake smile.

"Good morning again, dear Mama. I was merely discussing our final strategy for success in the upcoming election." He gave my shoulder a squeeze. He was getting on my last nerve.

"Raymond, you're not supposed to be in here bothering Brianna. She has plenty to keep her busy," she said, sweeping past him and coming right up to me. "However, dear, I did want to talk with you. It seems our appearance on the cable station and at school made quite an impact. I've gotten all sorts of calls and e-mails from people wanting to purchase your cupcakes."

She grinned so wide that I was filled with an awesome, warm, I'm-going-to-be-rich-before-high-school feeling.

"That's the good news. The scary news is that I've received orders for over five hundred cupcakes for Saturday evening Halloween parties. Even with the help of some of my staff here tomorrow morning, that's a mighty tall order. What do you say you and I sit and discuss how to work out the business side of this order and figure out how doable it is?"

My mind filled with recipes and dollar signs. Still, way, way, way in the back, a little voice wondered, *"What will Weasel do next?"*

I ☆ I ☆ I ☆ I

FOUR DAYS!

The election was in FOUR DAYS. Saturday, Sunday, Monday...then Tuesday, the Big Day!

Even though it was way too cold, Mrs. Nutmeg decided our class needed to go out and run off some excess energy. It was the first time since the girls and I were back talking that we'd gone outside.

Of course, we couldn't help talking about how everybody at the It Squad table had been throwing me the stank-eye. *Hmph!*

If that wasn't enough drama, as we were heading back inside from recess, Weasel appeared again to brighten my day.

"Remember what we talked about this morning, m'lady. Finally, the cool kids are listening to me. Don't you see? Once you're president, we'll own this school!"

I yanked my arm away from Weasel. "No more dirty tricks. If I win, I'll win fair and square."

His thin, wormy lips wriggled into a snarl. "If you don't do what I say, I'll make sure my mom kicks you out of the bakery. You'll never earn another dime for your tasty goodies. And we wouldn't want that now, would we?"

Then he was gone and I suddenly felt very cold inside my insulated coat. I didn't want to lose my chance to make cupcakes at Wetzel's Bakery, but I knew one thing for sure:

Weasel had to be stopped — for good!

35

The Minutemen
(Like the British soldiers who were ready in a minute, my girls jumped into action!)

"Brianna, you've got company."

I sat up with a start. My heart thudded in my chest. The family room was all dark and cozy. The curtains were closed and light from the next room cast shadows on everything—including the four people in front of me.

My mouth felt dry and for a moment I wondered if I'd dreamt that whole ugly scene with Weasel.

"Bree, sorry to wake you," Becks said. Becks was with Sara and Lauren. My mom was just behind them.

I looked past the girls to my mom. "I didn't know you'd gotten home already," I said. My voice was scratchy and sleepy-sounding. I sat up and tried to push the fog out of my brain.

"Well, Mrs. Wetzel called and told us about all the orders you got for your cupcakes. Your father and I decided we'd work with you, if you'd like, and help you get a head start on tomorrow's orders tonight. We're just so proud of our little businesswoman. Anything we can do to help, sweetie?"

Even though it was the uncoolest of uncool things one fifth grader could do in front of another, especially three others, I slid off the sofa and went and gave my mom a hug. She felt warm and comfy in her oversized Michigan State shirt and sweats, and I didn't want to let go.

She finally pulled away and said, "Go talk with your friends. We'll go over to the bakery and get started on the cupcakes after dinner."

Lauren twisted the knob to turn on the lamp by the sofa. Sara and Becks came and put an arm around me. Lauren said, "Ever since you told us at school what Weasel said, we've been trying to figure out a way to help."

I plopped back onto the sofa.

"I'm really glad my parents want to help with the cupcakes, but now, in a way, that makes it even worse. How can I tell them that Weasel is threatening to have me kicked out of his mom's bakery unless I let him destroy Jasmine Moon?" And how can I tell them that I've been cheating and scheming and being all notorious and that I have a dirty, rotten secret of my own that could shake the very foundation of our family!

"Well," said Sara, "we're here to help." She and Becks exchanged glances.

"What?" I said.

"Bree, you look, um, dazed," said Sara.

I felt dazed. "I was having this awful nightmare." I looked at Becks. "I was dreaming that Jasmine Moon knew MY other big secret."

"Really, it was so long ago, probably everybody has forgotten about it anyway. I don't think it would matter so much," Sara said.

"Are you kidding?" I asked. "I pooped in the sandbox. POOPED. IN. THE. SANDBOX! They called in the health department and we couldn't use the sandbox for, like, ever, after that. I almost shut down the school. No kid wants that kind of information to get out. Not EVER!"

Becks's eyes widened. "There isn't any proof of the,

um, sandbox incident, Bree. And believe me, I will never tell."

We all made the stink-face. It's an ugly memory, my friends, an ugly, ugly memory.

Lauren said, "Some secrets are better left untold."

We waited a second, then burst out laughing.

We hugged in a circle, and put our heads together.

I said, "This is it, ladies. We've got to end Weasel's reign of terror once and for all."

36
Rosie the Riveter at Your Service!

"Are you sure you want to do this?"

Becks looked at me with half-scared, half-hopeful brown eyes. I nodded. "I'm sure."

They'd all stayed at my house for dinner last night and helped me and my parents bake dozens and dozens of cupcakes. By the time I rode with my dad to drive them home, we were all falling asleep in the car. But like true friends, they all volunteered to get up at five the next morning and come with us to the bakery.

For hours, we all worked side by side at Wetzel's. I came up with a cupcake assembly line and everybody had a different job, from frosting to decorating to placing them on trays for storage on a tall rolling rack to be stored in the refrigerator.

Sara said, "Hey, we're like those 'Rosie the Riveter' ladies Mrs. Nutmeg told us about."

"We're nowhere near the river," Becks said.

We laughed. "No," I said, "Rosie the Riveter was like a symbol for women during World War II. So many of the men had to go to war that lots of places didn't have enough workers."

"So women started doing jobs that men had done. Now we're doing jobs that grown-ups usually do," Sara said.

"But we're doing it to help our friend," Lauren said.

Then we all pretended our butter knives, dipped in frosting, were power tools. We lifted them toward the skylight and shouted, "Keep riveting, ladies!"

"You guys, I came up with another cupcake recipe just for President Obama," I said.

Sara said, "I thought his favorite dessert was sweet potato pie."

"It is. So now I've created a sweet potato pie cupcake."

Everybody worked hard. And if somebody came up

with a better way to do things to make the work go faster, we did it. I couldn't help thinking about the school election. Don't think I'm being too mushy or anything, but running a good campaign is a lot like making a good cupcake. You try different ways, you use your best "ingredients," and you always, always, ALWAYS stick with the people who know you best—your friends and family.

(See, told you it was sort of mushy!)

By noon we were finished and began taste-testing all the cupcakes, including the President Obama–inspired sweet potato yummies. We were exhausted, but our insides were warm and delighted.

Mrs. Wetzel came over and hugged me twice, telling me how much her customers loved the new cupcakes.

"I'm so proud of how hard you've worked," she said. "Once the elections are over, we can discuss your school schedule and look at how you can earn money and keep working here."

Sara and Lauren had both glanced over at me; Becks had held her face over the cupcake she was eating, not daring to look up. They all knew what I was planning.

And they knew it could change everything.

Still, it had to be done!

✿ Brianna's Cookbook ✿

Sweet Potato Pie Cupcakes with Cream Cheese Frosting

2 cups all-purpose flour
1 cup white sugar
1 cup light brown sugar
2 cups boiled sweet potatoes
1 teaspoon baking powder
1 teaspoon baking soda
1 teaspoon salt
1 teaspoon lemon juice
1 cup melted butter
4 large eggs
See page 170 for frosting recipe.

Preheat oven to 350 degrees. Place the cupcake liners in a cupcake pan.

With a parent's help, peel two medium-sized sweet potatoes and boil until soft.

Now combine all the dry ingredients. You can use a mixer for 30 seconds at a low speed, then add the rest of the ingredients; add the sweet potatoes last—and slowly.

Use a tablespoon to fill cupcake liners 2/3 full.

Bake for 20 to 25 minutes or until you can slide a toothpick in and remove it clean.

Let cool for 10 minutes, then add your cream cheese frosting. Mmmm! If you see the president, tell him I've made a batch just for him!

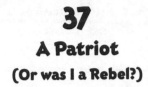

37
A Patriot
(Or was I a Rebel?)

The plan was simple:

Weasel had to be stopped!!!

So at 5:30 p.m. while he was at oboe practice, we did what we had to do.

We piled into Mrs. Wetzel's living room.

Now, when we talked about showing up to tell her that basically her only son was a dirty, rotten rat fink, we expected her to be shocked. To maybe order us out. Or at least tell me to get away and never show my face at Wetzel's Bakery again.

We were scared. I was petrified.

What we didn't expect, though, was for her to say,

"Why, that conniving little scoundrel. I should have known he was up to something!"

Bam! And just like that, it was on and poppin'. Mrs. W. was about to take down her little man with an evil plan of her own.

I told her he was planning to use some sort of embarrassing presentation at the Halloween carnival. "It's my fault," I said. "If I hadn't gotten so crazy about Jasmine Moon and kept acting like she was the enemy, maybe he wouldn't have made himself crazy with revenge schemes."

"I love my son, Brianna, but he's always had the tendency to go too far. Every now and then, he needs to be brought back to reality. And I think I have just the thing. He wants to see some embarrassing movies. I'll make sure that's exactly what he gets!"

I ☆ I ☆ I ☆ I

After some fast, pre-carnival trick-or-treating, we all headed to the school. Fifteen minutes later we were inside the school cafeteria, which had been transformed into a world of ghoulish adventure. Dr. Beelie was dressed as Frankenstein and wore Styrofoam bolts painted green sticking out of his neck. "Good evening, children, parents," he said.

Fog billowed from a tiny fog-making machine, and haunted house sounds filled the room from tiny, unseen speakers. It was all really fake, but at the same time, it was kinda cool. The little kids were screaming and running around.

Me? I could barely catch my breath because I knew what Mrs. W. was planning.

Becks was dressed like Frankenstein, too; Sara wore her horse-jumping outfit with a rubber mask, the kind that covers your head, with an ax through the skull; Lauren was a witch; and I was a vampire. Hey, when you're in fifth grade, you kinda don't get into the whole dress-up thing, but getting candy is cool, so you can't blow it off completely.

"There he is!" Sara said, pointing to a black knight. Even with a helmet on his head, he still looked like a weasel.

He carried a book bag over his shoulder. We all exchanged looks.

"He's got it," Sara said.

"I hope it's the right one," Becks said nervously.

I sighed. "We'll know soon enough."

"Have you officially withdrawn from the election, Brianna? I was just thinking, after that embarrassing failure in the trivia contest and then your pitiful plea to keep your friends, well, maybe you'd want to quit now and call the whole thing off."

Jasmine Moon.

She wore an Egyptian princess costume and was surrounded by a sad assortment of witches and ghosts.

"Oh, Jasmine, I didn't hear you arrive. You must have a broom with a quiet motor," Sara said.

"I'm not a witch, I'm an Egyptian princess," she snapped.

"No," said Lauren, "I'm pretty sure you're all witch."

"You guys," I said. I really wanted to avoid as much drama as possible.

"Like I need you standing up for me," said Jasmine Moon with a snort.

"Well...," I began, but she cut me off.

"I can't believe you went on TV and told everybody you didn't even care about the election. And to think everybody told me you were my only real competition.

And by the way, my parents are coming with a surprise. You're not the only one who can bake cupcakes. With the help of a pastry chef friend of my mom's, I've made some amazing cupcakes," she said. Then she nodded her head toward the back row of tables filled with platters of chips and dips and cookies and cupcakes. The school had placed an order at Wetzel's for my cupcakes. They sat in tiny rows on the table.

"Your little...whatever they are...won't look like anything next to my professionally made treats. I had real pastry chefs working with me. Not that Miss Delicious fraud you're so crazy about!"

So she's attacking Miss Delicious now, too? Is nothing sacred to this girl?

Tabitha Handy, my little geeky ex-stalker, gave me a little wave and nodded her head like we were in on some sort of secret. Jasmine Moon didn't see her, however. She was too busy flouncing off in another direction. Well, sure enough, about fifteen minutes later, her parents arrived. And they were carrying huge white boxes. I was so busy watching them open the huge boxes from a downtown Detroit bakery that I never heard Weasel come up behind me.

"M'lady, a word, please?" I looked over at Lauren. If her lip curled up any higher with disgust, it would wind up in her eyebrows. Weasel practically dragged me far enough away to whisper and not be overheard. With a big, slimy grin he said, "There's someone you need to meet."

Well, here comes Tabitha Handy. I thought about the weird little wave she'd given me earlier. What was going on?

"Tabitha has been my secret weapon," he said.

She bobbed her head like some crazed bobble-head doll. "It's true," she half hissed, half whispered. "You couldn't think I'd really help Jasmine Moon win over you, could you? From the start Weasel and I made this plan. I would never want anyone to get in your way, Brianna. I think you're sooooooo cool."

"You mean, you've been...been spying for Weasel?" I could barely ask the question.

She nodded. "Yep! Sorry about that stuff with the bogus presidential trivia answers. Jasmine Moon cooked up that idea to give you bad information and make you look bad in front of the school. She also hid that snake in the projection screen to freak you out."

It was like I couldn't breathe. I looked across the room at Becks. This was what I'd tried to turn her into. A big, fat, creepy spy. No wonder she couldn't do it. I was glad she didn't. I was going to have to bake a lot of Itsy-Bitsy Wild Banana Bites to make up for being such a lousy friend! We mingled—that's a fancy word for walking around and talking to a bunch of different people. We also danced together. If I'd taken a picture of Becks doing the robot, well, let's just say, for blackmail purposes, it might have been more destructive than the snot shot.

Later, Principal Beelie was onstage blah-blah-blahing about all the memories he had of his spookiest school Halloween parties. We knew this was it. He was going to have Weasel do the DVD, but instead of using what Principal Beelie wanted, Weasel had other plans.

The projection screen slid down behind the stage. Somehow Weasel wound up beside me.

He said, "You'll thank me later. This will show everyone what a hypocrite she is. Trying to get us kicked out of the competition for a harmless little second-grade prank, when she was willing to perform daring feats of treachery for a part in a fourth-grade play!"

"Weasel, get over yourself. You need to stop this! I

really don't want to be president if it means acting like a jerk."

But it was too late. On the screen, the images came to life. It started out with screaming kids and a haunted house set up right here in the school gym. *Woo-hoo-hoo* ghost sounds came from the speakers. A few kids laughed.

Then it changed. Now it looked like the camera was showing backstage at like an auditorium or something. You could see one girl and hear her talking to someone. Probably the kid recording her.

"The part of Cinderella should have been mine," said the girl in the costume.

The scene changed. This time it was Weasel. Any of us who knew him, knew this was in third grade when he thought he was a character from *Star Trek*. He was pedaling his bike as fast as he could up his driveway, and you could hear the person holding the camera ask him what was wrong.

He was crying and wailing, "I stole Missy Gardener's candy and she said she put a curse on it. Now there's a monster in my belly!"

Then the camera lens went down to the ground and . . .

249

aw, man. He was standing in a puddle of pee. Weasel had wet himself!

All the kids were like, "Oooo!" Then of course they laughed so hard I thought a few of them might wet themselves, too. Then I realized that Weasel's mom must have figured out what he was going to do and planted a nasty little lesson of her own.

Wow! Way to go, Mrs. W. You're the first diabolical mom I ever met!

Weasel ran across the cafeteria yelling, "How did that get on there? Who did this to me? *Moommmmmy!*"

Weasel started running out of the cafeteria even faster than he had on the screen. He was still making his getaway when Jasmine raced to the front of the room.

"Look!" she cried. "My parents just arrived. I made a surprise for everyone, my own cupcakes. It's my way of saying thank you all for being so kind to me."

Lauren said, "What do you think was on that tape? I wonder what dirt Weasel dug up on her."

I said, "I think we're better off not knowing."

While Jasmine Moon was sending everyone to the back to taste her cupcakes, I looked over at the trays that had carried my sweet potato cupcakes. They were almost empty. But they hadn't looked as fancy and professional as Jasmine's. Even across the room I could see the perfect peaks of frosting.

I tried not to feel bad, but I couldn't help it. Cupcakes were my thing. If she was good at that, too... well, it made me shake my head.

But then I started hearing noise coming from the back table. We moved closer.

"*Eeeeew!* How can it look so good, but taste so bad?"

Several kids held Jasmine's cupcakes away from them like they were covered in hair. Then Toady Todd slamdunked his into the garbage, and all the jocks around him did the same.

"That was gross!"

"Disgusting and gross!"

"It tastes like glue and bad breath!"

I sniffed, then took a bite of one. It smelled... weird. Like maybe the ingredients were cheap. Mrs. W. once told me that it didn't matter how beautiful your creation. "If you skimp on ingredients so you can splurge on making it look good, customers will know."

Jasmine Moon looked like an Egyptian princess who

was about to be fed to the crocodiles. Her face reddened, and with tears in her eyes, she raced from the room.

I looked at Sara and the others. "You guys, that's cold."

"It's her own fault!" Lauren said. We watched as several other kids slammed their Jasmine Moon cupcakes into the trash. Some kids even booed. BOOED! Can you "boo" a cupcake?

"Yeah, but, I don't know. That was just way harsh." I replied. "We should make sure she's okay."

We left the cafeteria through another set of doors, then raced around the corner. It took a minute or so to find Jasmine Moon. The black makeup around her eyes had smudged. She was crying. She looked like a sad raccoon.

"Jasmine...," I began.

"*Go away!* I don't need you here to make fun of me. I feel bad enough already."

"We didn't come for that. They were awfully mean to laugh at your cupcakes like that."

She looked at me with red eyes. "Leave me alone!" she shrieked, then pushed past us and down to another end of the hall. We ran to catch up.

"Jasmine, please. Look. We've been at each other since Day One. I never took the time to get to know you. You never took the time to get to know me. Hey, we both seem to like the same things."

Becks said, "At least two of the same things, elections and cupcakes."

I nodded. "No matter who wins, maybe we could, you know, start over?"

Well, that bit of niceness was like pouring the same kind of lighter fluid Dad used to start the barbecue on an already-flaming dessert. *Whoooomph!* Her eyes got wide and all the tears dried up. She looked like an angry, Egyptian raccoon. A raccoon with an attitude!

Giving me her stinkiest stank-eye, she crossed her arms over her chest and said:

"I know you are *not* trying to feel sorry for me! I don't need your sympathy and I don't need you." She walked up really close to me and wagged her finger in my face.

"It doesn't even matter that you stunk up the trivia contest. Zero points! How can anybody get zero? You got the same amount of points as my dog—and he wasn't even in the contest!"

Oh, now that's just rude!

"You need to get your finger out of my face," I said, taking a step toward her. I was mad now. Really, really mad.

"What are you going to do?" She stuck her face into mine. Before I could reply, Sara pulled me from one side, and Becks pulled the other.

"Forget her, Brianna, she's not worth it," Sara said.

"Let's just walk away," Becks said.

"You mean run away," Jasmine Moon sneered. "Face it, you've been scared of me since I got here. You're used to being Miss Popular here, and I've stolen it all from you. And when I win the election, nobody will ever think twice about you and your sad little cupcakes or whatever."

I blew out a sigh. The anger was gone. Always being mad at Jasmine Moon was making me tired and turning me into someone I didn't want to be.

"If winning means that much to you, Jasmine, then good luck. I think I'd make a great president, but I know I make an even better friend." I put my arms around my girls' necks. We started toward the cafeteria and then realized there were a bunch of kids in the hallway. Gretchen, Darrick, and a few other candidates were there, along with the Flowers and some kids from the fourth-grade hall.

A fourth grader shouted, "Jasmine Moon, that's cold, girl. Why're you treating Brianna that way?"

Gretchen rolled her eyes at Jasmine and said, "You think you're all that!"

She pushed past them all, flung open the doors, then...

❚ ☆ ❚ ☆ ❚ ☆ ❚

By the time we entered the cafeteria, we walked into a wall of stony stares and downright glares. What was up?

Dr. Beelie had tried to eject Weasel's edited film. But it looked like he'd managed to skip ahead and was showing some parts that Weasel's mom hadn't erased.

The DVD of Jasmine Moon and her dirty little backstage secret!

The girl holding the camera phone said:

"Jasmine, this is so awesome! We'll rip the thread out of all the stitches in her skirt and put a little tape on them.

When she gets onstage and starts moving around, her skirt will fall off!"

On the screen, you could see Jasmine on the floor with a big, flouncy skirt on her lap. She gave a thumbs-up to the camera and both girls started giggling. Then the DVD showed them putting itching powder in the girl's shoes, and a bunch of other rotten tricks.

Even Dr. Beelie had stopped his frantic quest to eject the DVD. Now he was just standing there with his mouth hanging open. The scene changed again on-screen. Now it was clearly during the show. The play was *Cinderella*. And JASMINE was the lead character! At first I had to lean in to hear what she was saying, until I realized it was Weasel. He was recording himself talking over the play.

"Watch this! Miss Moon did her dirty deeds to get into the play and thought she was off scot-free."

But she wasn't.

Instead, she took two steps in her beautiful *Cinderella* ball gown, then...oh no!

The whole bottom of the skirt came off!

Weasel's raspy whisper continued:

"It seems that the fifth-grade girl who got all itchy and scratchy when she starred in the performance the night before found out about a certain fourth grader's dirty trick. She decided to pay her young understudy back. Revenge is a dish best served cold!"

"Stop! Turn on the lights! Turn this off!" Dr. Beelie cried.

But it was too late for Jasmine Moon.

Much too late.

38
The Era of Reform

Sunday morning, after church, I went over to the Wetzels'. Mrs. W. invited me. Weasel sat in the kitchen with his head down.

"You okay?" I asked.

He looked at me with sad eyes. "How could you let her do this to me? I'll be ruined!"

"Stop your complaining," his mother said. "She didn't *let* me do anything. It serves you right. I've told you about playing your dirty tricks and trying to be slick. Maybe this will teach you. And Raymond, don't you have something else to say to Brianna?"

He lifted his head and said, "I'm sorry I threatened to kill your cupcake-baking dream."

His mom nudged him again.

"Oh, and sorry for threatening you and all that other stuff. I . . . I just wanted people to finally like me." He was whining.

"And you think that because you were willing to bend the rules, sneak around, turn friends against friends, and threaten others with losing out on their dreams that it would make the It kids like you?" Mrs. W. used her stern mother voice.

His head snapped up. For just a moment he got this crazy look in his eyes, like maybe being part of the It Squad was worth all the treachery and dirty schemes in the world. Then he looked from me to his mom, and the flashing in his eyes went flat.

"Nope. I guess not."

Mrs. Wetzel poured me a cup of coffee, and we discussed the amazing sales we'd done over the weekend. She said that I'd be welcome to bake at the bakery three times a week. Then she passed me two checks.

"The first one is for your first week of baking. The other is from just this weekend."

I couldn't believe what I was seeing.

My first step toward millionairedom—and charity. It felt good to be a mogul in training.

39

...With Liberty and Justice for All!

I awoke early. It was the Friday after the election.

A very big day.

Three days had passed and, like it or not, life went on.

On the way to the bathroom, I grabbed Pig Pig off the dresser and gave him a big shake.

"Pig Pig, what do you think?" I asked.

Pig Pig winked slyly. *Ahh, that Pig Pig.*

Before I could even finish brushing my teeth, I heard a phone ringing. Mom's cell. A few minutes later she was outside my bedroom door. "Need any help deciding what to wear? That was your aunt Tina on the phone."

"She's coming today?" I asked.

"She said you couldn't drag her away!"

Mom drove me to school, and even Katy told me to "have a good one, Squirt." But the "good one" wouldn't really start till the end of the day.

Dr. Beelie stood on one side of the stage and Miss Delicious stood on the other. Aunt Tina, Mom, and Dad were off to the side.

Three days after the election, and guess what?

"We are all here thanks to the kindness of our new president of the fifth grade... Brianna Justice!"

Yep, that's right.

My name is Brianna Justice, and I am president of the whole fifth grade!

Believe it or not, though, finding out I was president wasn't nearly as cool, and didn't feel nearly as awesome, as what was happening today.

Funny how that is, right? A few weeks ago, I figured the greatest thing in the world would be to have big money in my bank account *and* be class president. But here I was about to do something I'd never dreamed of, and it was starting to feel like the greatest thing ever.

Tuesday, the day of the election, I'd been so nervous, I thought I'd throw up or something. I wanted to act like winning was no big deal anymore, but inside I knew how much it still meant to me. What got me through the day, however, was the talk I'd had with Principal Beelie. I'd told him my plan—to help someone other than myself. He had been thrilled.

After lunch, we had an assembly. Dr. Beelie wore his George Washington outfit yet again. Then he congratulated all of us on a job well done. I thought I was going to faint.

"And the new president is...BRIANNA JUSTICE!"

For the rest of the day, I felt so many different things I was afraid all my emotions would push through my skin. I had won. I had made a plan. I'd followed it. I'd gotten in trouble for following it and almost lost my friends. So I made a new plan. And I followed it.

And now I was president.

"On behalf of Orchard Park's National Bank," said Miss Delicious, "I am proud to award a check for five hundred dollars, which the bank is giving to match the five-hundred-dollar personal donation of a truly incredible fifth grader, Miss B., Brianna Justice. Brianna has also spoken with her vice president, class treasurer, and the Student Advisory Board representative, and they all agreed to donate one thousand dollars out of their class's budget."

I'd been holding my breath. When she finished, I let out such a rush of air it must've caused a breeze. Knowing that we were doing a good thing, helping others, felt even more incredible than winning the election.

Miss Delicious was here at the request of the school and the bank to honor me with the biggest check ever. It was about five feet long and three feet tall. We were outside in front of the school and the camera crews were filming us. Mr. Tan and his crew were surrounded by reporters from newspapers and TV. Aunt Tina was scribbling in her notebook and... man, this was embarrassing, but I think she was crying a little.

And get this: Pinks 257 were in the background playing my song!!!

Why, you ask?

Because I had finally figured out what *Justice for All* should really mean: Doing the most good for the people who need it most. And finding a way to get everybody involved.

Principal Beelie said, "We are proud of the efforts of our new class president, **Brianna Justice.** She has proven herself a leader and an entrepreneur!"

He was talking about the money I was giving. It was a donation for the homeless family that had been living behind the school in the woods.

Miss Delicious waited for the applause to fade, then added, "It is my honor to donate an additional two thousand dollars toward helping the Rogers family get back on their feet."

Flashbulbs popped and we were mobbed by a swarm of **paparazzi**. Okay, maybe it was just a few local reporters, but some were from TV!

I'd earned more money than I could have imagined. At the bakery, Mrs. W. had given me two checks—one was for $500; the other was for $600. One check I donated; with the other, I put all but a hundred in the bank. The rest I was re-investing in "the business." Now I'd have to figure out what my business would be called.

Hmm...

Mom and Dad came over and gave me a big hug. "We're so proud of you, Brianna," they said.

Becks, Sara, and Lauren were wedged between the

camera people, waving. Dr. Beelie bent down to the microphone and said, "Brianna, would you like to say a few words?"

My girls gave me a big thumbs-up.

I took a deep breath and ignored the shaking in my knees. I handed the oversized check to the man from the bank, then I remembered a scene from one of my all-time favorite movies. Earth is being attacked by a bunch of aliens, and there was a scene when the president wanted to inspire the fighter pilots, so he stood up and gave a great speech.

I cleared my throat and tried to look as serious as if we were being attacked by killer aliens. I said:

"When I told Principal Beelie about my plan to donate part of my cupcake money, we talked about what had happened during the election. It didn't seem right that I was running around school, breaking rules and only interested in myself when there were people so close who needed... well, everything. And it also doesn't feel right that everyone is making such a big fuss about me doing something that, well, I guess I or anybody else in my place should be expected to do."

A slide show of American presidents raced through my

brain. For the past six weeks, Mrs. Nutmeg had jammed so much history about American presidents into our heads that I was constantly thinking about it. Most of the time, I figured she was doing it because she liked history better than fractions. (Even though we did lots of fractions, too!)

Anyway, after what I've been through with the election, I think Mrs. Nutmeg might've had another reason. I think she wanted us to learn that whether you're running for president of the United States or president of the whole fifth grade, you have choices to make—choices about who you are and what you can do for the people who vote for you.

I mean, history taught me that you can run a winning campaign but be a lousy president. In 1921, Warren G. Harding became the twenty-ninth president. He didn't campaign a lot, but when he did, he made promises that didn't make a lot of sense. He promised whatever group he was talking to whatever they wanted to hear.

Yeah, he won, but he wound up spending most of his time playing poker and golf and losing the White House china. (It's true; check your social studies book!)

Dr. Beelie's elbow nudged me and I realized I'd spazzed once again in front of the whole school. I was going to have to work on my public appearances. First I went all goofy at the trivia contest; now I'm standing in front of a crowd on a made-up stage on the school's front lawn with my mouth open, replaying the history of one of America's sorriest presidents.

"We as students should expect more of ourselves and be willing to help people in need even if we don't know them," I said.

I went on to tell the reporters we should all try to do what we could to help out and that if I got real good at selling cupcakes, I planned to do more.

For a second, there was so much clapping and hooting, I thought maybe I did just save the planet from dangerous aliens. Questions pelted me like sleet, but without the sting. Reporters from the *Detroit News* and *Detroit Free Press* alongside local reporters and TV people asked about the election, our school, the Rogers family, and my cupcake business. I tried to answer the best way I could, but like I said, the whole thing, everybody making so much fuss about something we should've been doing all along—well, it felt weird. When they finished, I was glad it was over.

I shook Principal Beelie's hand. Miss Delicious reached down and gave me a big hug.

"We're so proud of you," said Miss Delicious and Mrs. W.

"I'm kinda proud of me, too."

Aunt Tina came over and swept me into one of her world-famous hugs. "Baby Girl, you were amazing! Simply amazing!"

"It's no big deal."

Sara, Lauren, and Becks came over. Sara said, "No big deal? Are you kidding me? If Jasmine Moon had won, if she had earned all this extra money on her own time, do you think for a minute she'd have donated anything?" Jasmine Moon had been lying low since her big "performance," and I had done my best not to draw attention to her defeat. She already had enough to worry about without my help, and I was happy not to even be thinking about her for once.

I waved my hands. "Okay, okay, I get the point. Brianna Justice is remarkable, amazing, brilliant, gifted, and unique."

Laughing, Lauren added, "And don't forget humble!"

We all laughed.

Sara said, "I think it's so cool how when the bank found out about your donation, they chipped in."

"Miss Delicious, too!" said Becks.

"Well, I couldn't have done all this without my friends!"

Aunt Tina finished writing and closed her notepad. She gave me one of her thinking looks. "You know, now that you're a businesswoman, entrepreneur, and philanthropist..."

"A phila-hoo-*what*?" I said.

"Phil-an-thro-pist. A person who generously donates to the community or provides financial support for a given charity or cause," said Aunt Tina. "Anyway, I think it's time for you to start investing some of your money."

I couldn't help laughing. Aunt Tina's mind was always working. Before I could say more, she spotted Mom and said, "There's my baby sister. Let me go and praise her for being wise enough to allow me to influence her daughter's life!"

As we watched Aunt Tina go, Becks suddenly had her hand on her hip and crackled the cold air around us with a resounding triple-snap of her fingers that included honest-to-goodness neck rolling.

Did you just go there, Becks? Did you?

And as if she'd read my mind, she said, "Girl, I went there, saw the movie, and wrote the review!"

We all howled with laughter. Just so you know, that sort of thing was very *un*-Becks, but she always knew how to make us laugh!

"For real, girls, we know Brianna is a lot like her aunt, but maybe as our Woodhull Society moves forward, Miss Tina can be sort of a mentor to us all. Maybe we all could be better phil-an-thro-pists!"

Lauren nodded. "Sounds good to me."

We were still giggling over Becks's transformation into a Sassy Thing when I spotted Weasel. He was standing off to the side, behind a tree. I waved him over. Sara groaned. I nudged her.

"Hello, girls," Weasel said in a most un-weaselly tone. Was everybody getting all brand-new? Were my leadership skills working already? Was I changing the school one person at a time?

One day, I really will have power, money, fame, fortune... *waaa, haa, haa, ha!*

"Sorry about you getting embarrassed in front of the whole school," I said.

Lauren gave a little eye roll, but said, "Yeah, even a weasel like you doesn't deserve to get caught wetting his pants."

"Lauren!" said Sara.

But Weasel laughed a little.

"Yeah, well . . . maybe I did get a little carried away."

"Hey, Bree, think we can go to Wetzel's? I hear they've got some killer cupcakes." Sara was already moving down the sidewalk, grinning.

Weasel said, "I think we could get some good prices, m'ladies. I'm good friends with the chief cupcake chef."

The band was still playing:

> *No need to worry, she won't forget; Brianna Justice*
> *is your best bet!*
> *So cast your vote — no need to stall.*
> *A vote for Brianna means . . .*
> *Justice for all. Justice for all. Justice for all. Justice*
> *for aaaaaaalllllll!*

I ☆ I ☆ I ☆ I

Snow began to fall and we pulled our coats tighter around us. The sweet smell of the powdery snow gave me an idea.

I grinned and said, "I'm getting an idea for a new cupcake."

"Give us a hint?" Becks said.

"I'm thinking of a chocolate cupcake with chocolate chips inside..."

They all went, "*Mmmm!*"

"Then it would have white cream cheese frosting with white chocolate chips...mini white chocolate chips. I'll call it the Snow Angel."

Weasel's eyes started to shine. He said, "Ahhh, the Snow Angel. If you let me be your manager, I'll make it the best-loved cupcake in the world!"

We all let out a squeal and began to race away.

"Wait!" yelled Weasel. "I don't have to be your manager!"

But we kept running and laughing, with Weasel chasing us all the way to the bakery. I raced out ahead, wanting to lead, feeling good to be out in front. But I slowed down, just a bit. I didn't want to be too far ahead of my friends. Even Weasel. A good leader has to know when to run with the pack—and when to pull away.

As Lauren caught up, she shouted, "Last one there has to wash the pans!"

As I laughed with my friends, I realized I had learned

that the best recipe for success was one that included all the right ingredients: staying true to yourself, following a plan that makes sense, and trusting the ones you love. Now I knew that as long as I remembered that lesson, no matter what happened in any election or anything else, I couldn't lose.

I smiled as we ran to the bakery together, leaving a trail of powdered-sugar footprints behind.

Acknowledgments

I must say thank you to all the third, fourth, and fifth graders who listened to the progression of Brianna's story and gave me the encouragement to keep working to bring this character to life. To Mrs. Lewis's students at E. L. Norton Elementary School in Gwinnett County, Georgia; to Mr. Southworth's students at Virginia Shuman Young Elementary in Fort Lauderdale; and to Mrs. Oullette's students at John Young Elementary, thank you for listening and sharing your ideas (and eating many, many cupcakes as "Brianna" tested out her recipes).

Thank you, Julie Scheina. You stepped in and worked like a powerhouse to get this manuscript prepped and ready for surgery. It was my pleasure working with you on the final leg of *President*, and I appreciate your effort.

Without Jennifer Hunt's vision and leadership, *President of the Whole Fifth Grade* would have been a vastly different novel. Thanks, Jen, for your candor and insight. (And for letting me work with Julie Scheina.)

And thank you to my daughters, Lauren and Kenya, who continually provide me with ideas for young minds on the go!

Brianna navigates her toughest challenge yet... middle school!

President of the Whole Sixth Grade

SHERRI WINSTON

TURN THE PAGE FOR A SNEAK PEEK OF *PRESIDENT OF THE WHOLE SIXTH GRADE.*

1

How It All Began...

My name is Brianna Justice.

I am president of the whole sixth grade. If you are thinking that being class president means I'm popular, you're wrong. At least, you would've been—before everything that happened.

The truth is, getting chosen as class president in middle school was NOTHING like it was in elementary.

When we voted for class president in fifth grade, it was a big BIG deal. Win or lose, you knew it meant something—it mattered. Everybody was excited. Hearts were broken. Dreams were realized. It was...*amazing*.

In sixth grade? Yeah, "running" for class president meant having Mr. Galafinkis tap me on the shoulder and ask me to stay after class and fill out some paperwork. I think my only qualification is that I looked least likely to set a fire in the trash can. And I was one of the few kids who was shorter than him.

Anyway, being president of the whole sixth grade was an important job. It didn't matter whether or not you were popular. What mattered was getting the job done.

And the idea of failing started giving me nightmares.

See, every sixth grader at Blueberry Hills Middle School learned about THE BIG class trip to D.C. long before we started middle school. But somehow, despite about seventy-five of us paying our deposits the first week of school, our class was still twenty-five hundred dollars short.

Now it was up to me to turn my classmates into a lean, mean fund-raising machine, otherwise our big trip was not going to happen. And I didn't just *want* us to go—we *had* to go to D.C.

Why I HAD to help the sixth grade get to Washington, D.C.!

1. TO WIN! Each year, the leadership conference has a theme based on government—this year's theme was ancient Rome. We were going to compete with all the other schools to show how much we knew.

2. The most important magazine in the whole wide world, *Executive, Jr.*, was going to be at the conference. The magazine was doing workshops on leadership skills for business success, and offering tips for kids who wanted to start their own businesses. (I WAS ALREADY A BUSINESSWOMAN! And this could help me make my business even BIGGER!)

3. Our school had participated in this trip for twenty years and NO WAY would I be the first president of the whole sixth grade who FAILED. No way!

4. All of the class presidents had to give a speech. The winning speech would earn $1,000 for that school.

5. MOST IMPORTANT: Getting out of town would give me much-needed time with my girls!!!

So, as you can see, I had A LOT riding on this trip. And time was running out.

The whole thing started that one day. The day the museum lady came to our school...

2

The Ides of March

Wednesday, October 15

Rome was burning.

That's a metaphor. Maybe with a little hyperbole mixed in. It refers to a massive fire in ancient Rome that destroyed a lot of neighborhoods. It was rumored that this heartless emperor dude, Nero, played the violin while the city burned to the ground.

Living near Detroit, I knew a little bit about fire. Buildings sometimes got torched for no reason, although the city was trying to improve its image. The metaphor, about Rome burning, referred to me. My life. Only in reverse, because my world was burning up while the rest of my classmates fiddled, played, and joked around.

We were studying ancient civilizations, especially Rome, for Civics class. Preparation for learning modern government, our teacher, Mr. Galafinkis, said. We had to keep a journal comparing and contrasting our lives in middle school with life in ancient times.

At first, I thought that assignment was lame. However, it turned out that middle school had a *lot* in common with ancient civilization. Big egos...fighting for territory...weird clothes. The weak getting thrown to the lions for fun. And lots of **drama.**

Want to know a good vocabulary phrase for Civics?

The Ides of March.

Ancient Romans called the middle of each month the ides. Sometimes, like in the case of Julius Caesar, who found himself dead on March 15, 44 BC, the ides were bad luck. For me, on a particularly disagreeable day in the kingdom of sixth grade, I felt like I was suffering through the Ides of October. And in this case, the ides truly sucked.

Thanks to a laughable shortage of funds in the sixth-grade account, my class presidency was in BIG TROUBLE. Welcome to my world—*The Ides Edition*.

"Aw, girl, we've got plenty of time," cackled some sixth-grade deviant during what could only be described as "The Debacle." DEBACLE—totally a vocabulary word. It means awesomely bad failure.

The Cackler overheard me say how desperate I was to get started with fund-raising. I wanted to smack him in the head with my Civics book. We did not have plenty of time. The clock was ticking. Our trip was scheduled for Monday, December 8. That was less than eight weeks away. Plus, the money was due by December 1.

Which was why we invited today's speaker, a lady from the Henry Ford Museum who specialized in helping kids with fund-raising ideas. She came to help us brainstorm ideas. She was trying to help us raise twenty-five hundred dollars to get to D.C. However, after the way my fellow sixth graders behaved, I bet most of them couldn't even *spell* D.C.

If I could write what I really, REALLY wanted for my journalism assignment, here's what I'd say:

WAS THERE A MOOSE ON THE LOOSE?

(DETROIT)—The sixth graders had their first meeting of the school year today with Ms. Kenya Benson from the Henry Ford Museum in Greenfield Village. The purpose of the meeting was to discuss how to raise the $2,500 needed for our upcoming trip to Washington, D.C.

Sounds simple, right? So simple, even a sixth grader can do it? Apparently not. Like a lot of things in middle school, looks were deceiving.

Civics teacher and class trip advisor Mr. Galafinkis arranged for the students to meet with Ms. Benson because she specializes in school fund-raisers. But she said only a few words before the whole meeting got out of hand.

Maybe it was the macaroni surprise in the cafeteria. Maybe cafeteria food does something to turn students into mutants. Or maybe there's

(continued)

something to the rumor about that whole zombie virus thing. Maybe middle school water is filled with soul-sucking pathogens that turn perfectly decent sixth graders into soulless flesh-eaters who need to infect others in order to fit in.

Because something like that is the only explanation for what happened next. See, when the nice museum representative began speaking, a strange noise started coming from the back of the room. It was kind of a squawk and kind of a honk. It sounded like a moose. With a head cold.

Soon the sickly moose sounds were coming from everywhere, until finally the nice museum lady was eyeing the door, patting me on the shoulder, and saying, "Good luck!" She said it the same way she might say it to an astronaut being sent onto a cold, deadly planet to tame a nest of gooey aliens determined to destroy Earth.

Whatever possessed the kids to make the moose sounds, one thing is clear—THEY SUCK!

Thank you and leave me alone.

My three best friends and I had been so psyched about starting middle school. But then we got here and the whole world fell apart. Hyperbole again? Okay... maybe not the WHOLE-whole world fell apart. Sure was starting to feel that way, though.

The four of us were used to being in class together, eating lunch together, going to recess together. Now Becks and I were in honors classes, which were mostly in their own hall, unfortunately nicknamed "Lame Land" by the rest of the school. And the school was so big that even after six weeks, I *still* got lost.

That wasn't the worst part, though. Getting lost I could manage. It was the weirdness that drove me insane. Sometimes sixth grade felt so stupid I just wanted to punch myself in the face. Like, repeatedly!

Take Becks, my very best friend in the world. She used to wash her hands all the time because she was obsessed with germs. A pure hypochondriac—which means someone always afraid of getting sick. Now all she could talk about was wanting a boyfriend and wondering what it was like to get kissed.

And sweet, sweet Sara. It was as if every day was costume day. She said she was "expressing herself through the way she dressed." Two weeks into school, she started wearing only jeans and graphic tees. Now she was into pink. Like, *really* into pink. Seriously? *Seriously?*

As if that wasn't crazy enough, there was the whole size thing. In fifth grade, I was considered short. Okay, maybe I wasn't just *considered* short. I was—*am*— short. Or, excuse me, "vertically challenged." Anyway, so what? I could take a joke—I even had a T-shirt that said FUN SIZE. But in middle school, it was hard to just laugh it off.

Every day, and I do mean every single day, I got called everything from Baby to Itty-Bit. Random kids I barely knew would sometimes swoop me off my feet and twirl me around. Worse, Becks started doing it, too.

In grade school I was a lion. I roared like a lion. Queen of the jungle! However, with each passing day of middle school, I was more ly-ing than lion.

Why all the lying? Because middle school was the Land of Fake-Believe. Nobody in that place was honest about who they were or how they felt. Everything was some big fake-out. I told myself I was better than that. I didn't have to fake about anything.

At least, that was what I wanted to believe. It started small. Little lies, like laughing along with my friends even though I thought their video or Facebook post or whatever really wasn't all that funny.

Or pretending to be interested when everybody around me talked about getting with this boy or that girl, hundred-dollar sneakers, or who was kind of ratchet. Trust me, ratchet—not good.

Pretty soon I was faking more and more. Like, I faked that it didn't bother me that Sara and Becks seemed to be drifting away.

And I faked that I was cool with getting swooped around and called Baby Smurf. And when somebody fake-coughed and called me Nerd Girl or Dorkopolis just because I took honors classes, I faked like I didn't even care.

See what I mean? That was a lot of faking. I was getting pretty unhappy, but did I tell the truth and admit it? No! It was like admitting how I felt would make me look like even more of a loser.

When I climbed aboard the big, shuddering school bus after that dismal meeting, I was about done with middle school. I wondered if I could move into the Michigan woods and be homeschooled by wolves. (Well, since it was Michigan, maybe I could be schooled by Wolverines.) The bus shook again and my stomach grumbled. School buses were the worst. Especially when the driver looked at us like we were serial killers.

A lot of my classmates dressed like clones of their fave online stars. Girls with T-shirts pulled tight and held in back with rubber bands; boys wearing gym shoes that cost more than Daddy's car payment.

Kids pushed to get to their favorite seats. And as usual, everyone was being mega loud.

Sara handed me my clipboard and squeezed my shoulder.

Becks whispered, "Don't worry, Bree-Bree. It's just your first meeting with them. A lot of kids don't even know you yet."

Today's meeting was the first time a lot of the sixth grade had laid eyes on me. It had not gone as I'd diagrammed it on my trusty clipboard.

I plopped onto the bus seat and slid over to the window. Sara sat down beside me and immediately began whispering across the aisle to Becks about some boy who was "beyond cute." I couldn't help wondering where, exactly, on the map "beyond cute" was. I mean, did you take a right just past Handsome and go three blocks, crossing the Bridge of Attractiveness? I'm just saying.

Lauren sat in front of me, turned in her seat, and scoped out the action up and down the aisles. "Did you know that the world record for the largest bubble gum bubble is twenty inches in diameter?" She giggled. Then she blew a huge bubble and cracked it.

I couldn't help smiling at her. Lauren had always liked world records. At least she hadn't gone totally bonkers the way Sara and Becks had.

When did two of my best friends decide to become boy-crazed loonies? Was I next, destined to be the costar in their horror movie, *Creature from the Boy-Crazy Lagoon!*?

"Your friend," Sara said, knocking me out of my deep thoughts. I looked up and another kid from our elementary days moved into view. Raymond Wetzel. Nicknamed Weasel. His mother owned Wetzel's Bakery, where I worked as a cupcake chef. My whole life, all I'd wanted to do was be a millionaire cupcake baker.

Okay, maybe not my whole life. It might've only been since fourth grade. Still...

Weasel was a funny-looking kid who made weirdness a hobby. But somehow we'd become sort of friends. He raised his hand to wave. Before he had a chance to say a word to us, though, a large chunk of balled-up paper came sailing through the air.

PLUNK! Hit him right in his face. Ouch.

My mouth fell open. Several kids laughed and pointed.

I waited to see what Weasel would do, but he just looked at me, shrugged, then turned and trudged toward the front of the bus. Behind us, I could hear laughing, and one voice saying, "Yeah, you take yo' geeky behind back to the front!"

Between the moose calls, crazy moos, and being humiliated in front of the museum lady, I had had enough. I stomped into the aisle, Sara tugging at my sleeve.

I didn't recognize the paper-ball thrower, but it didn't matter. Somebody needed to set these kids straight.

"Hey!" I yelled. "Why don't you grow up?"

The boy sneered. He had mean, beady eyes and wore the kind of expression that said he was no stranger to detention.

"Awwww, shut up . . . *Jelly Bean*!" he said.

That was followed by a chorus of laughter. Sara gasped, Becks's eyes got huge behind her glasses, and Lauren immediately jumped to her feet.

Jelly Bean. Just because some eighth grader had decided my electric-blue pants and candy-apple-red Converse were too bright and said, "Dang, girl! You look like a big jelly bean," now it was a thing. I'm sure people thought if they said it, I was supposed to be all embarrassed.

Well, I had a surprise waiting for my would-be tormentors. The next person to try to shame me with that stupid nickname was going to learn a thing or two about Brianna Diane Justice.

I removed a ginormous plastic bag filled with jelly beans from my backpack. I opened it and scooped a handful into my mouth.

I chomped them.

I grinned with multicolored globs of jelly-bean goo stuck in my teeth like a psycho jelly-bean fiend.

My heart hammered in my chest. I didn't really *want* to be a psycho jelly-bean fiend, but, see, that was the thing about middle school. Sometimes it made you do stuff that you just couldn't explain. When I'd finally swallowed enough sugary candy not to choke, I said:

"Maybe I do dress like a jelly bean, but I can always buy new clothes. I know you're not trying to talk about how anybody looks! Looking like what would happen if Frankenstein and Bigfoot had a baby!" The back of the bus erupted into laughter.

With way more confidence than I felt, I spun around, flinging the zippered plastic bag like some sort of crazy flag.

A stampede of jelly-bean-hungry sugar freaks drowned out the "oh snap" and "man, she told you" chorus that filled the air.

I slumped back against my seat. I thought shutting down a bully would make me feel better. It kinda did, but it also didn't. The bus driver yelled for everyone to be quiet. Then the old yellow school bus staggered into traffic.

Beyond the window, trees rushed past. Their giant green Afros of summer leaves had transformed into an array of dappled red and gold 'dos. As the bus's tires flung gravel and grit across the cement road beneath us, Sara whispered, "Brianna, you're *soooooo* brave."

I wanted to believe her. I really did. But I was afraid that the truth was, I was just a much better faker than she knew. Maybe I was the biggest fake of all.